RAGING RIVER

Advance praise for *Raging River*

"*Raging River* is an incredible story that completely captivated me. It made me feel I was living the adventure. If you like adventure, it's a must read."

— Tao Berman, three-time world record holder and Pre-Worlds Champion

"*Raging River* is a captivating story of outdoor adventure, survival and the trials of friendship. I enjoyed it thoroughly, and can't wait to share it with my family."

— Steve Markle, Outdoor Adventure River Specialists

"I was lucky to find a passion for kayaking at an early age. *Raging River* captures the excitement and love for the sport that has kept me motivated to chase my dreams. This book really takes it to the extreme."

— David Ford, eleven-time Canadian National Champion in whitewater slalom kayaking, 1999 World Champion, three-time Olympian and eight-time World Cup medalist

"Like those on a well-planned trip who find themselves on an unplanned adventure, readers of *Raging River* are first seduced into caring about Jake Evans and his band of river runners, then compelled to watch them carried into the maw of mistakes in a deep canyon wilderness. All the while, Pam Withers's compassionate, intelligent voice instructs us effortlessly on the life of river guides, the physics of rivers wild, and the details of the dangers of wildlife and waterfalls. It is a terrifying and satisfying read."

— Richard Bangs, founder of the Sobek Expeditions international rafting company and author of *The Lost River*, and other books

"This is a great story with lots of twists and turns. It's a page-turner for paddlers and non-paddlers alike."

— Charlie Walbridge, author of the *American Canoe Association's River Safety Anthology*, and other books

"An adventure story that will captivate the imagination of every youth who loves the outdoors."

— Margaret Langford, three-time Olympian and member of the Canadian Whitewater Kayak Team

RAGING RIVER

Pam Withers

Dedicated to George Withers, my father-in-law,
and Jeremy, my son.

Text copyright © 2003 by Pam Withers
Walrus Books

Fourth Printing 2006

Edited by Carolyn Bateman
Proofread by Elizabeth Salomons
Cover and interior design by Roberta Batchelor
Cover photograph by Randy Lincks/Masterfile
Printed and bound in Canada

National Library of Canada Cataloguing in Publication Data

Withers, Pam
  Raging river / Pam Withers.

  (Take it to the extreme 1)
  ISBN 1-55285-510-4
  ISBN 978-1-55285-510-2

  1. Rafting (Sports)--Juvenile fiction. I. Title. II. Series:
Withers, Pam. Take it to the extreme ; 1.
PS8595.I8453R63 2003   JC813'.6   C2003-911062-1

The publisher acknowledges the support of the Canada Council for
the Arts and the Cultural Services Branch of the Government of British
Columbia for our publishing program. We acknowledge the financial
support of the Government of Canada through the Book Publishing

At Whitecap Books we are committed to protecting the environment and to the responsible use
of natural resources. We are acting on this commitment by working with suppliers and printers
to phase out our use of paper produced from ancient forests. This book is printed by Webcom on
100% post-consumer recycled paper, processed chlorine free and printed with vegetable based
inks. We are working with Markets Initiative (www.oldgrowthfree.com) on this project.

Contents

1   The Apprentice

Angry river water slapped at the cold walls of the canyon as Jake Evans pulled on the oars of his inflatable rubber raft. He was sweating to maneuver the stupid thing into a pool of calm water before taking on the last churning rapid. He turned his weary gaze to the jagged, mid-river boulder just downstream: a massive finger that rose defiantly from the river's depths.

"Devil's Finger," he muttered, shivering. Jake swiveled to study the dark clouds beginning to choke out what little light was left of this spring day and told himself that one more treacherous rapid wasn't a big deal after a full day's training.

He shivered again as he ran a hand down the rubbery neoprene of his wetsuit, the one he'd finally bought after saving a month's allowance and some of his weekend wages. It was adult-sized — a bit baggy for a fifteen-year-old — but he figured his lanky body came close enough to filling it. At least it kept out the brisk wind and icy waves. Jake breathed in the damp fog and smell of wet forest and sighed. A part of him wanted to climb out of the raft and curl up on a log to sleep. Another part wanted to light a stick of dynamite and toss it at Devil's Finger. That way, he'd blast two complicated paths through a rapid into one smooth cascade and a "yahoo!" sort of ride to the day's finish.

River raft guides, of course — even trainees like himself — weren't supposed to think like that. They were supposed to be totally into nature and challenge. And most days, Jake was. He just needed a quick injection of energy and courage right now to get around this ugly boulder and slalom neatly through the jumble of rocks and water below it. Then he could pull up full of confidence to where his boss, Nancy Sheppard, stood. He imagined his tall, lean, thirty-year-old supervisor stepping up to the raft to shake his hand, and instantly promoting him from trainee to junior guide.

Jake shrugged off his silly reverie and got ready to dip his oars back into the current. He would take the fork to the left of the evil finger, angle his raft from the riverbank to just above the boulder, then swivel into the long, foam-laced tongue of water that wrapped itself around the rock. Nancy, whose years of experience had earned her head-guide status at this adventure tour company in Chilliwack, British Columbia, Canada, had told him to steer left here at high water. He could see Nancy on the shore far below, a distant figure holding a rescue rope and standing beside a pile of trainees' rafts. He relaxed his grip. They'd made it; so would he.

With a surge of confidence, he plunged his oars into the current and whipped his craft around into the choppy whitewater. But as the raft shot out of its resting eddy, its front lifted too high on a surf wave and skidded sideways. Jake's pulse quickened as a downstream wall of gray water rose to cut off his view of the boulder. The canyon walls all around him began tilting at crazy angles. As his craft spun out of control toward the face of the finger, Jake shifted on his plank seat and dug his oars in harder to straighten out and avoid the blinding spray of water ricocheting off the stone's pocked face. Next, he launched himself into the front compartment and frantically pressed himself against the bottom of the boat, trying to force it down. It was the only way he could think of to stop the raft wrapping itself around the boulder like a dishrag. The last thing he remembered was his shoulder smashing into the unyielding edge of Devil's Finger as the boat slid up against its left face, hesitated, and, with a shudder, twisted and folded over Jake's sinking body.

Nancy told him later that she'd never seen a raft

spiral and fold quite like that. Nor had she ever seen an overturned, runaway raft pinball down a rapid so smoothly, picking its path intelligently, running on autopilot while its stunned driver remained temporarily trapped underneath.

What Jake did remember was this: Nancy and the trainees lifting him out of a frosty pool well below where he meant to end up. If that wasn't embarrassing enough, his next sight, as he sat crouched on the cold riverbank, was of Peter Montpetit, his childhood friend-turned-jerk. Peter, arms crossed and sneering down at him, was framed by half a dozen kayak racers attending an elite training camp just downstream of the rafters' take-out point. Jake hadn't yet made the Canadian whitewater kayak team this year and had missed this weekend's session for lack of money. Now here he was, washed up at their training camp with a bruised shoulder and torn wetsuit — a failed raft guide, staring up into a ring of superior faces.

"... And if he doesn't live," Peter was saying in his clear, booming voice, blond curls wagging, "I know for certain that his will provides for that wetsuit to be donated to my club in Seattle."

"*Seattle*," thought Jake wearily. Peter's father had nabbed a fancy job in the States a few years ago, and Peter had been able to join the U.S. kayak team because his dad was a U.S. citizen. The novelty of the situation still hadn't worn off, and Peter liked to lord his new credentials over his former Canadian team-mates. Still, they didn't seem to mind, welcoming him back on his weekend visits to their kayak training site near Chilliwack, just north of Seattle over the U.S.–Canadian border.

"Back off," Jake responded as Nancy helped him to his feet. "I'm okay." He eyed the rocky shore and avoided the eyes of both the kayakers and his fellow raft-guide trainees. "Where's my raft?"

"The gang'll load it onto the bus trailer in a minute. It's in perfect condition, amazingly enough," Nancy replied. "The trainees and I did a merry chase after your raft, you know, but it wasn't until the kayakers joined in that we managed to pull it out. And there you were, floating comfortably alongside, one arm tucked into a side rope, hiding like Houdini. Kate has jogged back for the bus and here we all are."

Kate Johnston, Nancy's short, pudgy assistant, had gel-spiked hair and more energy than a hamster on an exercise wheel. She was helping with trainee evalua-tions today. Peter and the other racers, instead of moving off, hung around as Nancy continued. Jake felt a hot patch creep up his neck and into his face.

"Seriously, Jake, you made all the right decisions after you got turned around. You prevented a more dangerous splat against the upstream side of the boulder. We're not into losing a trainee or an expen-sive raft like that, right gang?" Nancy turned to the rest of the guide trainees — two girls, five guys, all older than Jake — who gave her a thumbs-up.

"Right!" they murmured.

"So, Jake, just another day in the life of a guide. You demonstrated good instincts and no doubt learned about the power needed to paddle across a flooding river. You'll make a good raft guide yet, but it's time to get you into dry clothes and call it a day. Especially since it's starting to rain." Turning to Peter and the rest of the kayakers, she added, "Thanks again for your help."

Peter separated himself from the group and sidled up to Jake. "Is the shoulder okay?" he asked, putting out a tentative hand to touch Jake's arm.

"It's bruised, that's all," said Jake, shrugging off Peter's touch. He'd seen his old friend shift from his hot-jock mode to concern in an eye blink a few too many times, and he wasn't taken in. "Won't stop me from hammering you next race." He hoped his grin didn't resemble a grimace.

"In your kayak or your raft?" Peter shot back. The Canadian team members guffawed on cue and pressed around Peter like groupies at a rock concert as the blond hotshot spun around and headed back to the kayak camp.

Jake gave the kayakers a mock salute with his good shoulder and followed Nancy's troop back to the raft company's old repainted school bus as raindrops turned into fat splatters. He shook his head as Nancy offered him a towel and fleece jacket, but accepted them once he was inside the bus. From a window, he watched Peter stuff his head of yellow curls — the ones the girls always fell for — into his gold-speckled helmet and lower himself smoothly into his tight-fitting kayak. Rain pelted down as the slalom racers maneuvered their smart boats neatly between poles hung on wires over the fast-moving river.

Of all the places to wash up, why at the kayakers' feet? Jake thought, burying his helmeted head in his hands. Many of them acted stuck-up around him, or maybe he just imagined it because they all had nicer boats than he did and they'd made the team and he hadn't yet. But Peter had definitely become a first-class creep. Jake raised his face and looked out the bus window just in time to see Peter form a perfect pirouette around a candy-striped slalom pole. Jake felt envy course through his shivering body and ooze out through holes in his rubber wetsuit boots. To Jake, Peter had it all: good looks, confidence, athletic talent — and money.

Only a few years earlier, the two had been inseparable. They'd grown up next door to each other, Jake's father an airplane mechanic and Peter's dad a float-plane pilot for logging camps. Then things had gone bad between Jake's mother and father, and Jake's father had packed his bags and left late one Saturday night after the worst fight ever. Jake could still hear the sound of a plate smashing on the tiled floor in the kitchen — and the unnatural quiet in the house after the front door had slammed. Jake's dad had disappeared without so much as a letter to his family since. That same month, Peter's dad had landed the job flying commercial airliners out of Seattle.

The two families' circumstances had diverged radically after that. In the end, Jake had lost not only a father, but his best buddy. Peter's more flush circumstances, along with his incredible success on the U.S. kayaking scene, had gone straight to his head. The two had lost contact for a while, and the friendship had died. Then, a few months ago, Peter had started showing up every weekend at Chilliwack's world-class training site, which was better than anything Seattle had, to boost his skills before U.S. Nationals. And the Canadian team members acted like he was a newly crowned king or something. Peter just didn't seem to see how arrogant he'd become and it really burned Jake's butt. Sometimes he wanted to pummel Peter blind; other times, he wanted to run away from the sound of Peter's exuberant voice and the shattered memories of good times they forced on him.

As far as Jake could tell, all Peter had to do these days was ask his parents, and they'd buy him a state-of-the-art kayak, a new wetsuit, even a trip to Costa Rica for pre-season training. Jake never asked his mother for money because he knew she didn't have much of it. Deadbeat Dads are hard to take to court when you can't find them. He was lucky to have an old race kayak to paddle and a weekend job that paid for rides to occasional races. Special coaching sessions were out of reach until he made the Canadian team and got some funding. Peter, on the other hand, probably had more weekly spending money than Jake could earn monthly between his paper route and weekends at the rafting company.

Jake had only just missed a slot on the Canadian team during a competition the previous weekend. It was a slot he wanted more than anything in the world. Lack of funds and his rafting job had kept him from attending this weekend's training, but he figured he could still clinch a berth at the next team trials. If he did, he'd be going to the National Championships less than two months away.

Even with the funding he'd get for making the Canadian team, he knew he'd have to save hard to afford the trip to Ontario for the Nationals. Jake's brow furrowed and he huddled into the hard, slick bus seat. Man, it was cold in here. How was he going to pay what he still owed for his wetsuit and save for Nationals at the same time? The wetsuit, of course, had been an essential purchase for his weekend rafting job — where he might still, despite today's big disaster, get promoted. Although too young to qualify as a full-fledged guide, Jake worked like a dog at the adventure tour company. He figured that was why Nancy encouraged him toward the junior guide slot, where he could guide in an emergency and develop boat-handling skills useful for when he turned eighteen. Besides, she'd told him he was the best cook in western Canada. It was a good thing Jake's mother had taught him a few things about making meals before taking her second, evening job. All those nights of making dinners for his younger sister had given him a useful skill for a raft company's Boy Friday. Jake knew Peter couldn't boil an egg if his life depended on it.

"Jake, what are you dreaming about?" Nancy called out as she leaped into the driver's seat and shut the front doors against the late afternoon shower. "Get out of those wet clothes before I have to assign the girls to strip you." The female trainees sitting up front giggled like sixth graders at recess, and deeper laughter and catcalls came from the guys, who were busy throwing the last of the oars and paddles into the muddy aisle of the bus. Jake obediently peeled his damp body out of the damaged wetsuit, after deciding he could mend the shoulder tear. Sometimes he felt an outsider in this group of older students, but he still liked their good-humored company and particularly enjoyed the after-work arm wrestling contests they got up to at headquarters. He could beat every one of the females except for Nancy, and one or two of the guys on a good day.

Jake watched Nancy move her lean but powerful frame down the bus aisle, checking gear. Guides and trainees fell silent as she passed. Though her weather-beaten face, tangle of black hair, and stern, dark eyes made her anything but good looking, Jake liked Nancy's relaxed manner. She had a quirky, deadpan humor off the river and she'd been raft guiding so long she was a legend in British Columbia. Jake often found himself wondering what it must be like to have guided that long — since the Dark Ages. Nancy Sheppard was simply the toughest, most perceptive person he knew. He liked working hard for her.

She also held the key to his two most immediate goals: the extra weekend work he had asked for so he could put money toward the Nationals, and the two weeks off he was counting on her giving him if he qualified to go. He hadn't asked Nancy about Nationals yet, of course. With Nancy, you didn't need to say much. Somehow, she always knew what was on your mind. That's probably why she had stood up for him in front of Peter and the team back there.

Jake squirmed again as he remembered looking up at that circle of kayakers' grins as he crawled out of the river. Next training camp, he'd be one of the kayakers, he vowed, not an unexpected, washed-up observer. And next weekend at team trials, he'd qualify for the team, whatever the slalom course had in store. It would be his last chance. He'd hardly registered this thought when he felt the bus take a sharp swerve, heard Nancy's piercing scream, and found his half-dressed body plunging off the bus seat. It slid heavily up the aisle until his head drove into the gearshift box.

2   Sam's Adventure Tours

"**G**ood thing you hadn't taken off your helmet yet," Nancy said, voice shaking a little as she unbuckled her seat belt and leaned over Jake. "You're not having a very good day, are you? Any more of this and we'll ditch the evening first-aid courses and just inspect your body every hour."

Jake grunted and pulled himself into a crouching position. Face burning, he forced a smile and shuffled back to his seat.

"Everyone else fine?" Nancy called out as she glanced around, swung the bus doors open, and stepped out into the downpour. Jake rubbed his steamed-up window to peer out at a small jumble of rocks the rain had unleashed from a muddy cliff. Good thing Nancy had braked fast. Everyone filed off to help Nancy clear the roadway and Jake peeled the rest of his wetsuit off and raced to dress before they returned.

"Nothing serious," his favorite guide, eighteen-year-old Vinay Sharma, reported as they returned to their seats. "At least the rain has cleaned some of the mud off the bus — probably saved Jake a bus wash."

Jake, his fingers massaging his sore shoulder, mumbled, "Right."

"Let's save him supper duties by hitting the local pizza joint," suggested Kate, toweling her wet blue and blonde spikes. Kate's well-known love of food and talking often had her ducking Nancy's orders to supervise raft unloading so she could help Jake in the rafting headquarters' kitchen. But Nancy always seemed to let Kate "The Mouth" Johnston do what she liked. Maybe she'd even approve Kate's pizza idea.

"Pizza!" the students chanted.

Nancy smiled as she headed for Sam's, formally known as Sam's Adventure Tours. "Let's," she agreed, "after the rafts are put away."

Half an hour later, Jake's tic-tac-toe game with Vinay on the bus's foggy windows was cut short as the vehicle pulled into the blinding brightness of Sam Miller's giant garage. Like airplane passengers arriving at a long-awaited destination, the students jumped from their seats and stampeded for the bus door.

Like a well-trained fire brigade, they grabbed paddles, oars, oar frames, life jackets, and bailing buckets and passed them hand over hand to their proper cupboards with a din that made Jake's ears ring.

To Jake, Sam's garage was more than a weekly workplace. It was his empire, his getaway, his private retreat. It was all his, from the jumble of books in the windowsill, to the tool bench Nancy had let him build in the workshop. Sure, Sam owned it, the guides shared it, and layers of laughter and laundry filled it up every weekend. But as the company's hard-working gofer, who often had the place to himself while the guides were on the river, Jake considered it his. If it weren't for school — only two more weeks, hurray! — and kayak training, he'd live here full time. Then he could be a true member of Sam's noisy extended family, with no stuck-up racers to put him down and fat paychecks to put toward anything he wanted.

As it was, of course, his pay would barely let him join the guides for pizza. That's why he usually preferred to whip up something delicious from the kitchenette's cupboards, which Nancy kept well stocked for their unofficial chef. That way, by the time Vinay was ready to give him a ride to his house on the other side of Chilliwack on Sunday nights, Jake was all filled up with good food and warm friendship, ready to face a week in his other life, with its schoolyard cliques and long, lonely evenings. Each evening after his mother had placed a kiss on his forehead and left for work, he had only his homework and sister Alyson for company.

When Alyson was busy with her friends, he'd steer

his bike for the club boathouse down by the river, where he would tug his green kayak from the racks and take it for a spin, sometimes in the company of other club members, who alone shared his dreams of glory. Jake wasn't avoiding other kids, exactly. He was just responding to a strong need to work super-hard and do super-well at a sport that had commanded his attention from the first moment he'd seen it on television. Whitewater kayaking, more than any sport, girl, or hobby he'd met, had a firm clamp on Jake's heart. He was a slave to its excitement and possibilities, and he dared to aim for the highest levels. Not through sharing training secrets with team members — he didn't fit in with them and their more expensive kayaks — but through self-discipline and being more determined than anyone could guess.

The sound of the bus firing up prompted Jake to scramble for the bus door, which Vinay had closed with a teasing grin.

"Come on, Vinay. Not funny!" he protested as Kate charged up the bus aisle to tickle Vinay long enough for Nancy to pry the doors open.

Pizza. Mmm. He could hardly wait. Pizza would make him a bit late getting home. He'd try to finish up a little homework by flashlight in Vinay's car on the way there. But, well, pizza was precisely what he needed.

Before the bus could back out of the garage, Jake

saw Sam step through the side door and signal to Nancy. His giant bulk and bright blue eyes, set off by a full red beard, were tough to miss. Nancy cut the bus's engine and stepped out to trot over to the company owner. Jake observed their animated hand gestures and pulled down his window hoping to overhear snatches of their conversation as they moved to the old desk in the corner that served as Nancy's "office."

"What's up, do you think?" Jake asked Vinay. His friend rubbed at the shadow of a moustache sprouting above his thin lips.

"Dunno," he replied, then cracked his knuckles. "You're our usual spy, being here during the day. Maybe he's booked enough people for a trip up north this spring. It didn't go last year, but I heard he was trying to drum one up again. What a grunt that would be — working day and night for spoiled, out-of-shape customers who think they're adventurers."

Jake laughed. "Always so subtle and positive, Vinay." He stole another look at Sam and his manager and let his mind drift. A long trip in northern British Columbia would mean wild rapids, nightly campfires, and maybe bears, moose, and tasty salmon.

"You wouldn't go?" he asked Vinay.

"Sure, I'd go for the bucks. But it would be a total hassle compared with day trips. Anyway, Nancy would pick the strongest, most experienced guides.

No way would she go for a kid trainee, if that's what you're thinking. Or even me, with my two years' experience, wuss bod, and occasional temper."

"*Occasional* temper?" Jake teased, ignoring the rest. But it bugged him big-time that Vinay was probably right about neither of them having a chance, even though neither of them knew what long raft trips on northern rivers were all about.

"Nancy'll pick Ron Gabanna for his body-builder physique and his seven years of experience raft guiding in the Amazon, you know, plus he's an amazing kayaker," Vinay continued. "Kate 'The Mouth' is her pet, and Angus Cohen'll get asked for sure. Now *there's* a sweet kayaker for you, Jake. He's totally awesome picking routes in heavy stuff from his raft, too. Anyhoo, y'think he and Nancy might have somethin' going?"

"Who cares?" Jake muttered as Sam, huffing to lift his frame aboard the bus just ahead of Nancy, gained the final step and boomed, "Well, hello guys and gals. I hear we're doing a pizza run! Don't mind if I join you."

Half an hour later, over his third piece of double cheese and pepperoni, Jake felt Nancy's eyes on him. He didn't turn to look, couldn't exactly see her, but he knew she was studying him. Why? he wondered. Do I have tomato sauce dribbling down my chin? Is it 'cause I blew my big chance today? Or am I finally growing a beard? Eventually, he just had to turn her way, but as soon as their eyes met, she looked away and busied herself with her salad and pizza. She obviously wasn't about to let him know what she was thinking. If only Vinay was right about the big trip and wrong about Nancy choosing only senior guides. But who was he kidding? He wasn't even a junior guide yet. All he could do was patch rafts, fix buses, and make grub. Good grub. Yes, maybe he had a chance. He looked Nancy's way again. She smiled at him just as Sam stood, the legs of his chair screeching against the café's greasy floor. Wiping bits of pineapple from his mass of beard, Sam beamed at the group.

"I want to congratulate you all on a fine day on the river," he began. "I understand Nancy and Kate put you through all the day's exercises, not to mention some rescue practice for our poor Jake."

The team laughed. Jake cringed.

"As you know, this is the fifth and final week of your training, and I think the near-flood conditions were excellent for evaluating quick responses and confidence. Nancy, Kate, and I are pleased to announce that all of you have passed your courses, and even Jake here is being promoted from trainee to junior guide, although we do hope he and Devil's Finger will do less sparring in the future."

More laughter and cheers, and some pounding on

the table. "Nancy will be issuing your certificates next week, and on behalf of Sam's Adventure Tours, I'd like to thank you for training with us. Nancy will be setting up new work schedules over the next week. If you have any special requests, feel free *not* to drop them on her desk."

A few chuckles.

"I'm also pleased tonight to share with you some very exciting news. As some of you may know, our company has in the past run multi-day trips near Prince George on the Cattibone River. Just today I've booked the minimum number of passengers required to run this eight-day trip and can confirm that Nancy will be leading the expedition in three weeks. We've had great response from our new color brochures and will be taking three rafts and three raft guides, plus two safety kayakers."

Vinay elbowed Jake and said in a low voice, "Safety kayakers are for peeling rafts off rocks and retrieving paddles and customers gone overboard."

"I know, you idiot. Shhh."

"We'll be notifying staff selected for this trip over the next few days," Sam continued. Clapping filled the room. Sam beamed again.

Cool and double-cool, thought Jake. Lucky guides who get to go. Especially if he was the one chosen to cook for them.

"And finally, I am pleased to inform you that I've

decided to pick up the tab for tonight's pizza and drinks."

Jake gulped down his cola and tapped his fingers impatiently on the checkered tablecloth. "It's up to you, Nancy," he thought, willing her to read his mind. "Do I or don't I make the best meals around, and can I or can't I patch rafts and fix buses in any conditions? Am I in or out?"

"You're on the list," she whispered later as the guides filed back to the bus. "*If* you want to go, and *if* you'll cook. It'll be double your usual pay."

"If I *want* to?" Jake replied, spinning around to hug her. He couldn't believe his nerve, hugging his stern boss. But Nancy just laughed.

"I take it that's a yes? Angus Cohen and Ron Gabanna will be in kayaks. Kate, Vinay, and I will guide the rafts. I'll have you do the safety talk for the passengers, too — you need the practice. By the way, three of the passengers have moved here recently from India, so I hope Vinay will help them feel welcome."

Vinay the diplomat, Jake mused. Just 'cause he'd immigrated to Canada from India when he was ten, Nancy thought he'd be the one to play host to some newcomers? So that's how the skinny brat had made the list? Great for me, thought Jake, who enjoyed Vinay's company, but he hoped the passengers wouldn't be what Vinay liked to call "flabby fake adventurers."

3   Fast and Clean

Every nerve in his body tingled as Jake locked his bike up outside the club boathouse early the following Saturday morning. Any other day, he'd have regarded the river as rather festive-looking, with endless strands of wire strung across it between trees, gaily striped pairs of poles (called "gates") hung from them at just the right width to let a kayak pass through with a whisper of an angle. Painted numbers above each gate showed the proper sequence. Some dangled over whitecapped waves, others directed racers away from surface-breaking rocks, and still others swung over eddies: calm pools where the water flowed briefly in reverse swirls.

Jake stood on the chilly riverbank, hands stuffed into his jean pockets, studying each gate with an intensity usually reserved for notes the night before a big test. Even with three years of whitewater slalom racing under his belt, he couldn't look at a racecourse without his heart pounding and a shiver shooting up his spine. In two hours, the sun — he hoped — would begin to warm his chilled bones and the riverbank would fill with nervous kayak racers, stern judges, and noisy spectators. In seven hours, everyone would know who had and hadn't made the Canadian team — in other words, who would get funding before Nationals. Would he be one of them? Jake gnawed on a thumbnail as he walked up and down the river, memorizing the tricky moves each gate required.

He'd go just left of that rock there, straight down the center chute, and accelerate into Gate 18 with a radical downstream lean. And then . . . Jake chewed his lip and stared at a particularly nasty whirlpool, which kayakers and rafters call "holes." Oh my god, how was he supposed to keep out of that hole without missing the next gate? It was hidden in heavy currents behind a mid-river rock the size of a Volkswagen Beetle. "Muscle, finesse, and a touch of luck," he murmured to himself.

Jake vowed he would touch no poles during his two required runs down the twenty-five-gate course. Not when every touch exacted a two-second penalty on a roughly two-and-a-half-minute course. At his level, that's all it would take to be knocked out of the running. Missing a gate, of course, would add fifty seconds to his time. Unthinkable! So, just two runs down this less-than-a-quarter-mile section of rock-choked rapids. He could do it. He had to do it to make the team. He pulled his hands from his jean pockets, rubbed them together, and smoothed his thick brown hair.

On his fifth stroll down the course, confidence building, Jake jumped as a car swung off the road and stopped just inches from his behind.

"Well, good morning!" came a shout from the passenger side of the silver BMW. "Jake, my man, it's your big day, eh? Way to scout before anyone gets here. Good strategy."

"Hi Peter, hi Mrs. Montpetit," Jake responded, nodding at Peter's mother in the driver's seat. "Nice car."

"Thank you, Jake," replied Laura Montpetit, cutting the engine, swinging her long legs out of the car and searching for a patch of even ground to place her high heels. "We just bought it. I'm still getting the hang of it." Her quaffed blonde hair framed a warm smile as she removed her sunglasses and reached fingertips toward Jake.

"So nice to see you again. How are your mother and your sister, Alyson? We miss our Chilliwack days, you know." Jake thought he glimpsed a smirk on Peter's face as he proceeded to unload his boat from the BMW's car racks. "They're great, thanks."

"And today's race is your team trials? Nice for Peter that he's allowed to compete in them just for practice. I'm sure you'll do splendidly, Jake. I'd stay to watch but I'm due to fly to New York in a few hours. Flight attendant's life, you know. Good luck, Jake. And have fun, Peter. So nice to see you boys together again. I'll see you Sunday night when your friend brings you home, honey. Fast and clean, guys. That's how you say go fast, without getting penalties for touching the poles, right?"

"You got it. Bye, Mom."

"Bye, Mrs. Montpetit," Jake said.

Peter turned to Jake and shuffled his feet. "So, want to walk the course together, old pal?"

"Just finished, actually. Go for it. There's a nasty hole between Gates 22 and 23. Need really strong strokes to make 23 without going over."

"Hey, coach. Thanks for the warning. Oh, one of the guys told me you're doing the Cattibone next month. Is that by kayak or raft?" Peter's voice taunted.

Jake, heading for the boathouse, spun around, hesitated, and replied in a measured tone, "Raft."

"In a raft," Peter repeated, his pitch a little high for Jake's liking. "Now why would Sam take a runt like you?"

"Because I can cook."

"Cook, schmook. You're getting *paid* to do a week of whitewater on the Cattibone? Do you have any idea how wild it is, how dangerous the rapids are? You could get killed. I've heard there's a ninety-five-mile-long canyon with Class 4 and 5 rapids. That's

Class 4 and 5 on a 1 to 5 scale — and 5, may I remind you, kills folks way better than you or me! I've heard there's a thirty-foot-high waterfall no one has ever paddled. That river will be *screeching high* in July. Your rafting company shouldn't even run a commercial trip on it, let alone with a novice like you."

Jake smiled. It was so rare to have a hold over Peter, he chose to rub it in with silence.

"What would I *give* to kayak it," Peter continued, throwing his hands up to the sky as if he was in drama class. "You 'n' me, Jake, could do a first run of the falls, get our photos in a magazine." He grinned, then grabbed his gear bag, dumped its contents onto his kayak, and peeled down to his shorts.

"You're insane," Jake exploded. "You wouldn't dare jump a thirty-foot waterfall in your kayak, and I'm not even *going* in a kayak. This is work, for Chrissake. It's pocket money for the Nationals. And has anyone ever told you that you talk too much?" He spun around and stomped toward the boathouse. Why was Peter in such a good mood, anyway?

"Mmm, quite regularly," Peter replied. "But listen up, because I have some quite startling news for you. You will pretend to be delighted, Jake Evans, even if you aren't, because you are such a polite boy. When would you like this juicy item?"

"Never." Jake paused but kept his back to Peter as he registered the sound of Peter zipping up his wetsuit and pulling on his paddling jacket.

"My parents are signed up for that exclusive northern raft trip of yours. They booked it through their travel agent. They wanted an exotic way to spend their anniversary. I just found out."

Jake's shoes sprouted roots as he watched an ugly cloud cast a shadow on the boathouse ahead. A backcountry raft trip was a rich pilot's and flight attendant's idea of fun? He turned the news over in his mind and steeled himself to turn around and shrug.

"Okay, that's nice. I'll treat them well and make sure they have a great time. Don't worry about them."

"But that's not the point!" Peter snapped while wriggling into his sprayskirt. The rubberized miniskirt fit snugly around his waist, ready to snap around his kayak's cockpit rim.

"Then what *is* the point?" Jake growled.

Peter grinned, climbed into his boat, secured the sprayskirt, and pushed away from shore. Jake's tummy tightened like a fist. Peter took three long, smooth strokes and capsized. Hanging upside-down under water, he took his time positioning his paddle for a roll. Finally, he drew a perfect arc across the surface and spun back upright, smirking at Jake as rivulets of water sparkled down his face and life jacket.

"I'm going too. I've talked them into it! Nifty, hey? You 'n' me and the Cattibone."

Jake's body went numb, his mouth opened, but no words came out. He swallowed. "In your kayak?"

Peter's smile dimmed as he stroked back to shore. "Nah, Sam wouldn't hear of it. I'm a U.S. team member and all, and he says no way, he won't take that kind of responsibility. Can you believe it? I'm more likely to save his clients' fat asses with my kayak than his guides are to keep me safe in his rubber arks. But anyway, no, I'm just going to be one of your pampered passengers — except maybe we can sleep in the same tent so we don't disturb my parents' honeymoon. Whatd'ya say? Do you ever sleep with passengers?"

Jake forced himself to stop grinding his teeth and ordered his jaw and face muscles to relax. Peter, a master at one-upping his rivals, had pulled off the coup of the season. But maybe it wouldn't be so bad after all. He'd be company. "So," he replied with forced cheerfulness, "we'll have an adventure together. But right now I have more important stuff to think about." He pulled himself up tall and, determined not to give Peter a chance to say more, marched toward the boathouse, almost slamming into Moses Wilson on the way. He'd competed against Moses, who lived on a native reserve near Prince George, in the past.

"Hi, Moses. Racers' meeting in an hour, right?"

Moses nodded and carried on to the river with no change of expression or gait.

"Well, see if I let you in on any moves," thought Jake, mystified as always by Moses' aloofness.

"He never talks to anyone, unless he's giving them bad advice to help his own placing," Peter called out from his eddy as the husky, broad-shouldered boy disappeared up the river, scribbling in a notepad as he studied the gates. "Plus he takes wacky risks to make up for being slow."

"Yeah, and since when have you and the guys ever *tried* to talk to him?" Jake shot back. "Or maybe it's good advice and you just can't make it work for you."

"My, we are crabby today, aren't we? Careful you don't end up an outsider like him, Jake old buddy." Peter aimed a paddle full of water in Jake's direction, but Jake was long gone.

The sunrays Jake had hoped for by race time were playing hide and seek as he secured his bib displaying his race number, pulled on his sprayskirt, and launched his boat a few yards upstream of the man coordinating the start.

"Junior men's division," a loudspeaker squawked. "Good luck to you, boys."

Moses' broad back blocked his view of the starter until Moses turned around and said in a deep voice, "See you at the bottom, Jake. Good luck."

"Good luck to you, Moses."

"Three, two, one, *go!*" Moses was off, and it was Jake's turn to place his kayak's tail into the waiting hands of the starter. He rested his paddle on his lap, splashed some river water on his face and sucked in long, deep breaths as he visualized each of the first moves on the course.

"Three, two, one, *go!*" Jake peeled out through his own spray and quickly aced the first few gates. As pushier waves began battering his boat, he pulled harder on his paddle, applying sure, steady strokes, vaguely aware of gaining on Moses, who was battling it out in the next section. He swooped into an eddy gate halfway down the course, startled for a second by the sight of a blue jay perched on a low branch over the river.

"Craw!" it protested, preening its colorful wings.

"That's a good omen," Jake told himself between hard breaths. The bird called out again as, like Jake, it lifted and flashed up the eddy's border, arched gracefully, and flew downstream to the final, most challenging section.

Just ahead now lay that horrendous hole — a deep, bubbling crater of whitewater that required a detour to the left. Jake gritted his teeth and ignored the burning sensation in his arm muscles as he weaved from gate to gate like a child connecting the dotted lines of a picture. "Paddle — through — the — pain," he recited with such concentration that he failed to register a whistle and shouts from people on shore. Digging his paddle into the foamy waves, he dropped past the enormous hole, slid uneasily through Gate 23, and spun around to tackle the second-to-last gate. But before he could swish through it, an empty kayak rocketed out of the depths of the hole and skidded softly into his lap. Jake froze, trying to register what was happening. That's when he heard someone shout: "Swimmer on the course!"

Jake took one hand off his paddle to shove the front of the unmanned kayak to a safety boater, who'd muscled upstream from the finish line. At the same time, he glanced upstream to see the monster hole spit Moses out. The ugly gash on Moses' forehead, his contorted face, and the fact that Jake had passed by without even seeing him, could only mean that Moses had been thrashed deeply in that hole for some time. Jake hesitated as Moses, gasping for breath, floated into him and grabbed hold of Jake's stern. Just as quickly, a man on shore tossed a rescue rope that landed neatly on Moses' shoulder. Moses grabbed hold.

"Nice aim," Jake thought and looked up to see tall, bearded Angus Cohen — the kayaker and raft guide from Sam's Adventure Tours — reel Moses in, a look of concern on his boyish face.

"Sorry, Jake; you'll get another run for interference,

of course," said Angus with a nod.

Peter, panting as he slid down the riverbank into Angus, blurted out, "Hey, Moses, if you can't control your boat, then give the rest of us more clearance, okay?"

"Peter!" Jake hissed. "You've got no right …"

"Jake," Moses said with a wince. "I'm sorry I messed up your run. Really, I'm sorry."

"I know," Jake replied, tossing Peter a withering look. Angus, always thoughtful and responsible, helped Moses out of the water, checked him over for injuries, and patted him on the back. "A-okay, kid, except for that shallow cut on your forehead."

He turned to Jake, rested his strong, hairy arm on Jake's shoulder, and said, "Wish you hadn't scared away my blue jay. I wasn't finished with him."

In answer to Jake's inquisitive look, the gentle giant pulled a notepad from his pocket to reveal a stunning sketch of the bird. Jake remembered then that Angus was a keen birder and an amateur artist.

"My good luck omen," said Jake.

"I don't doubt it," Angus replied as he grinned, turned, and strode up the river bank, sketchbook in hand and mop of curls bobbing in the breeze.

"I'm going to need all the luck I can get," Jake thought, crushed that his perfect first run was now disqualified, and wondering where he would find the strength for two, rather than just one, more.

Still, he raised his chin and dug in on the next sprint out of the start. He ended up retracing his route with perfect precision. Two down, bonus run still to go.

"Gotta give this one everything I've got," he mumbled aloud as he dragged his leaden feet toward the start again, lowered his kayak from his shoulder, and rubbed his aching biceps.

"That won't be enough," came a voice behind him. Jake turned to see Moses, eyes fixed on the ground. "You're looking tired, Jake." Moses lifted his face, marked by the new welt, and locked guarded brown eyes on Jake's briefly, before lowering his head again. His wet hair stuck out at all angles from the drainage holes in his kayak helmet.

"You gotta clip the edge of that hole or you won't make the team. It'll shave several seconds off your time, and line you up just right for Gate 23. The other guys won't risk it. I didn't pull it off, but you can. You wanna make the team or not?"

Without waiting for an answer, he shuffled off, jets of water squeezing out from holes in his neoprene socks.

Jake stared at the river waves to his right and put his hands over his helmet's ear holes to block out the cheers of the crowd. For a moment, he could hear nothing but a ringing in his ears and the chirping of dozens of sparrows in the trees overhead. He raised his eyes and tried to make out what the sparrows were trying to tell him. Then he tightened the strap on his helmet, cinched his life jacket closer around his waist, and shoehorned himself into his kayak.

This time, his muscles started burning even before he'd completed the top section. This time, he felt like the river had turned to molasses. Upstream turns were now slow-motion efforts, not spins-on-a-dime. Poles reached out like sticky fingers for his boat, making him duck and lean and breathe in short gasps. Even his elbows hurt as he pointed his bow toward the final section. Deaf to the cheers of the crowd, Jake stroked directly for the drooling mouth of the hole, just as Moses had advised, eyes locked on the gate below it, and recruited every cell in his body to help him stay upright. He slid through the fibrillating bulge of water and felt an invisible hand shove him hard through Gate 23. Moses should be a coach, he thought as his heart raced with excitement. He tied a neat loop around Gate 24, and with his last milligram of strength, pulled through Gate 25 and across the finish line.

Face lowered to his deck, limp arms trailing in the water, eyes shut tight, he whispered, "Done."

Minutes later, giant water splashes failed to revive him as Peter dived into the river, surfaced, and grabbed Jake's boat to shake it back and forth.

"Jake, you reckless, goon. You made the team!"

4   Heading North

Dust was creeping in through every crevice of the bus, making Jake's eyes burn and his throat feel like sandpaper. Worse, his rocking stomach was beginning to feel like it harbored a rotten egg. Nancy ignored the heavily rutted road and slowed down for nothing. Her long brown hair was matted to the back of the driver's seat, and her intent, tanned face rarely left the road ahead. She'd been driving like that for two days.

"We'll be at the Cattibone River sometime tonight," she'd told them earlier as endless miles of evergreen trees, occasionally broken by a scrubby farm, flashed by Jake's smudged window.

Angus Cohen, oblivious to his surroundings, sat near the front of the bus, curls nearly brushing a patch of peeling paint on the ceiling of the bus. Jake guessed him to be around six-foot-seven. He was studying an illustrated bird book, as if anything feathered would come within a mile of this rattletrap school bus hurtling down this empty road.

Kate 'The Mouth' and Vinay were sprawled on their stomachs full-length across from each other on rear seats, playing chess on a tiny magnetic board atop a pile of bulging canvas bags. Kate was bantering nonstop about the history of the Cattibone as she took turns moving pawns. Vinay, with a pale, drawn face, looked as uncomfortable as Jake did. He kept cracking his knuckles and glancing at a nearby window as if he might need to bolt there any moment. Behind Kate and Vinay, stacks of paddles vibrated deafeningly, and the acrid smell of the tightly bundled rubber rafts in the rear of the bus added to Jake's misery.

Ron Gabanna sat alone as always, gazing out a window, a sullen expression on his face, long, unkempt blond hair spilling over his bare, knotted shoulders. Two silver earrings sparkled in the sunlight. He pressed a can of beer, hidden from Nancy in a paper bag, against his grizzled chin and took a practiced swig. His mottled nose complemented red cheeks, one sporting a scar, and bloodshot blue eyes. Jake wondered how he could consume anything, let alone a warm beer.

"Nancy, um, when's our next stop?" Jake asked.

"Needing a little boy's room again?" she teased.

"No, just wondering."

"We'll be off this highway and onto a rough road within half an hour. That'll take us through the Cattibone Indian Reserve, if they allow us to pass, and we'll be at our riverside campsite an hour before dark. Otherwise, we have to drive another few hours and we'll get there around bedtime."

"*This* is no highway," snorted Vinay. "And why *wouldn't* the Reserve let us through?"

"Because it's within their rights." Nancy's voice had an edge to it.

"Checkmate," Vinay announced, stroking the prickly black hairs under his nose.

Kate groaned and rolled onto her back. "As usual."

Jake produced a set of playing cards from his pocket and waved them at Vinay. Anything to take his mind off the rotten egg and dust and make Vinay stop cracking his knuckles. Vinay snapped the chess set shut and staggered up the aisle to Jake, pulling himself forward on the empty seat backs as the bus pitched and shook.

Two games of War later, Jake and Vinay looked up as Nancy, true to her word, turned onto a track that was sure to loosen any bolts left on the bus. Jake wondered how Ron's and Angus's kayaks, cradled in a metal frame atop the bus's roof racks, were managing to stay tied down. He pictured Peter flying up with his parents in a small plane that served drinks and lunch. Although he and Peter would be sharing a tent —

which meant they'd better start trying to get along again — Jake hoped Peter would realize that this trip was work for him, and he'd have limited time to play or explore.

He wondered what the clients would be like. Nancy had said they included a doctor and his family recently moved to Vancouver from India, and four New Zealand dentists who had been backpacking in California all spring, two of them brothers. Dentists clearly make too much money, Jake decided. Then, of course, there was Laura and Richard Montpetit, and Peter. That made ten paying passengers plus Jake as camp slave, to be carried by three rafts guided by Nancy, Kate, and Vinay. With Ron and Angus trailing along in kayaks, that made a group of sixteen.

The bus lurched and slowed as Nancy changed gears to enter a small community. Vinay lowered their dusty window so they could see out. Jake counted a dozen shabby white houses, piles of cast-off belongings on their sagging porches. Laughing children ran in all directions, tugging on sheets hung from sagging wash lines. A skinny dog stood on its hind legs to lick a wood spit over a massive firepit. Jake's eyes followed two other mutts chasing each other; then he cocked his head to examine two kayaks tucked up against one of the houses. Further back, chattering women with armloads of foil-covered pans were filing into a sturdily built log hall beside a small wooden church.

Despite the chaos and rundown look of the place, Jake sensed a warmth here. A middle-aged man with a leathery face approached the parked bus.

"Good evening. I'm George from the Band office. You're Nancy?" The accent was strange to Jake's ears.

"That's right," Nancy replied. "We're launching our eight-day Cattibone trip the day after tomorrow. I spoke with you about hiring a shuttle driver from the Reserve to drive our bus to The Forks, where we'll finish our trip. And may we have permission to take the road through the Reserve this afternoon?"

The man stepped aboard and cast his deep-set eyes on the piles of gear, then on each crew member in turn. His eyes fastened at length on Ron, who had hidden his beer can. The older man rubbed his chin and finally turned to Nancy, jerking his head toward the log hall. After Nancy had disappeared into the hall with him, Ron shuffled off the bus to a nearby outhouse. Jake squinted at the little outbuilding, which tilted crazily to one side, a slice of corrugated roof broken off, paint peeling, and a single rusty hinge holding the door in its frame. He decided he'd wait for the campsite facilities.

Soon Ron re-entered the bus with cupped hands and cast a menacing grin about before heading toward Vinay. He dropped a large, hairy spider in Vinay's lap, and the boy shrank against Jake with a pinched face and tried to smile. Ron delivered a massive belly laugh so close to Vinay's face that even Jake felt overpowered by his beer breath. Then Ron pinched his large, calloused fingers around a leg of the fleeing spider and tossed it out the open window.

"You think that one's scary?" he boomed. "You should see 'em in the Amazon!"

Jake, thankful that Ron had not chosen to pick on him, giggled in unison with Kate and elbowed Vinay to do the same. Just then, Nancy and her host emerged from the log building and shook hands.

"Everything is worked out," she announced with a smile as she climbed into the driver's seat holding a grocery bag. "We've even been given a few loaves of bannock for supper tonight." As the aroma of the rich, freshly baked bread reached Jake, his stomach instantly mended. Kate skipped up the aisle to yank one squat loaf from the bag and broke it into pieces for everyone. As Jake munched on his, he noticed a husky teenaged boy pause in the log center's doorway and study the bus briefly. Although the boy retreated quickly into shadows, Jake could have sworn it was Moses.

An hour later, the bus arrived at a solitary campsite beside the mighty Cattibone. Jake and Vinay clambered down the steps of the bus with stiff limbs and stood captivated. Neither had ever witnessed a river of such volume or power. Gray waves pushed and pulsed downstream as far as they could see. The opposite shore was a full thirty yards' reach. Jake walked to the edge of the river and plunged his hand in.

"Yikes, cold!" he said. The other guides laughed.

"What do you think our wetsuits are for?" asked Kate. "Now help me unload the food cartons so we can fuel up for unloading the rest of this trash heap."

Even Ron, the silent, moody one, grunted approval for Jake's beef chili that evening.

"Not bad, kid," he said. Eaten with the fresh bannock, it was delicious, thought Jake: a nice reward for their long drive.

Nancy, her shiny dark hair in a ponytail that reached her waist, squatted beside the fire. "Here's what's happening," she said, poking the smoldering coals with a stick. "Tonight we'll check all the equipment, inflate the rafts, clean the bus, and straighten up the campsite. At the crack of dawn tomorrow, I'll drive to Prince George Airport to pick up our clients. We'll get back here just as two fellows from the Reserve arrive to take the empty bus away. We've paid them to drive it down to The Forks, a bridge one hundred seventy-five miles downstream of here, where our trip ends. That's the only bridge between here and our take-out point, where we'll arrive in nine days. We'll launch here before noon."

"Sounds complicated," Vinay offered with a yawn. "What I need is some sleep. A week of it will do. I just finished exams, you know. I'd also like a back rub from a beautiful woman, but we forgot to bring one along."

"Well, I wouldn't have offered anyway!" Kate said with a mock sulk and merry laugh as they doused the campfire and crawled into their tents.

5   Welcome to the Cattibone

"Pssst!" Peter said, beckoning to Jake an hour after the bus had arrived with all the clients the next morning. Jake was busy carrying gear to the designated launch site on the riverbank, but he paused, turned, and followed Peter's pointed finger to the edge of the forest nearby.

He spotted a doe and her fawn peering at the group, long legs ready to bolt back into the shrubbery.

"So?" Jake said, turning back to his packing.

Peter couldn't believe it. How could Jake not be impressed? How could he not appreciate sighting wild animals in the wilderness? When had Jake turned so grumpy? Peter wondered. He'd gotten worse, rather than better, since they'd been paddling together on weekends again — on weekends, that is, that he wasn't skipping out of valuable training time to work at this outfit of geeky or geriatric guides. Jake just wasn't taking his training seriously anymore, even if he had squeaked onto the Canadian team the other weekend.

If he'd just work less, train more, and *try* to be nice, maybe he'd be more fun to be around. Like he was back when they'd lived next door to each other. Back when they, their parents, and Alyson would all go on picnics together, or Jake's dad would show the boys how to tinker with engines. So his parents had split. Lots of kids go through that. They don't all turn it into a permanent grumpfest. Or take it out on everyone and everything — even on does and fawns catching the morning sun in the wild.

Peter knew he was making all the effort to get along again and wondered why. It was a real prize of a vacation, even if they weren't in their kayaks.

Peter tried again. "So how often do you see that? It's wild!"

"Peter, I know you don't see deer running down the streets of Seattle every day, but they're really pretty common on raft trips in northern British Columbia." As if Peter didn't know Jake had never been here before. "Let me know when you see a cougar, moose, or bear, okay?"

"Are there cougars, moose, and bears here?" Peter asked, jumping up in excitement. How cool would *that* be? He touched the strap of his camera.

"Yes, but they're unlikely to bother us unless we're sloppy with where we leave our food, or do side hikes without making noise for warning," Jake said. "And since you're our unofficial noisemaker, that won't be a problem. I'm delivering the safety talk in a little while, so listen up for more information then."

See? Impossible! Peter shrugged and slumped away. He checked his new camera to make sure his batteries were still charged, then disappeared up the path along the river, determined to capture bigger game.

When he returned, Jake was busy strapping gear into a raft with the East Indian boy, so Peter plunked himself down in a camp chair that hadn't been loaded yet and eavesdropped on their conversation.

"So, any paying passengers on this trip who have done whitewater before?" Jake was asking Vinay.

"Not a one of them, as usual, which is why we're called guides and paid exorbitant fees, I suppose. Unless you count Peter, who seems to think that rubber is a lower life form than the plastic from which kayaks are made."

Peter bristled but forced himself not to jump up.

"And what do you make of Dr. Joshi and his family?"

Ha! thought Peter. Good one, Jake. Devious, old buddy. 'Cause not a soul in the group had failed to notice Vinay's moonstruck face when Dr. Sunil Joshi's seventeen-year-old daughter had stepped off the bus. Pathetic, really. As if he stood a chance. Neeta was, by any standards, a beauty queen. That scary-looking muscle-bound Ron guide had already nicknamed her "the Indian goddess." And Jake had told Peter, shortly after his arrival that morning and out of earshot of Nancy, how Vinay had been grumbling, "No self-respecting guide should be told to do cross-cultural babysitting for no extra pay."

"They're very quiet," Vinay was saying to Jake. "Dr. Joshi and Neeta speak fluent English, the mother, Anita, less so. Both women are very shy and will hardly say a word in any language. All I've gotten out of Neeta is that she plans to study photography at an art school next year. I expect they'll loosen up. If not, it'll be a long eight days in my boat. I understand you're riding in front of Nancy on the food barge."

"Yeah, well, just because the oar raft carries the food doesn't mean I have any access to it between meals. And I suppose it's not a big deal, but I don't like being stuck in the freight car with the boss breathing down my neck all day."

"Well, someone has to be in the oar raft, and no doubt Nancy will trade you for someone else when she gets bored with looking at the back of your ugly head. Cheer up, slave. You'll be a full guide some day." And off Vinay sauntered to help the Joshis with their gear.

"So, Jake," Peter spoke up, pleased to see his friend jump at the unexpected interruption. "When do we get to hear this speech you're making?"

Half an hour later, the day was clear and warm, and small whitecaps danced playfully beside the tethered rafts at the group's launch site. Birds chirped from every branch of the surrounding trees, driving the guide Peter had nicknamed "Bird Man" to distraction as he and Nancy lashed ice chests, a first-aid kit, spare oars, and piles of waterproof bags into the oar raft. Peter circled them, shooting pictures.

"Whoa," Angus said as Nancy tossed him one large bag. "Warn me before you toss heavy ones, Musclewoman." Peter watched Nancy's eyes twinkle as she threw the next bag even harder.

Peter moved down the beach and saw Ron, shirtless as ever to display his sculpted form, drag each of the two kayaks by the grab loops on their bows, leaving a trail through the dirt to the river's edge. Lucky guy, Peter thought. Sam should have let me paddle. I reckon I'm as good as Ron. He turned and looked for Jake, only to find him and Vinay — having *finally* finished the dishes — joining Angus and Nancy to strap down the last of the gear bags.

Peter thought about offering to help but figured they wouldn't let him anyway. So he sat down on the beach and searched for good skipping rocks. What a boring morning. He'd even walked up and down the shore to scout the rapids ahead. Nothing there, really. When were they going to get to the good stuff?

"Good thing you remember Nancy's knot-tying course better than me. I have too many thumbs," Vinay was grumping to Jake.

"And too little patience," Jake suggested, patting him on the back.

"Peter!"

Kate, the chunky lady with the punk haircut was lining up the passengers to be fitted for wetsuits and life jackets. He had his own wetsuit, which fitted him handsomely, thank you very much. He wasn't allowed to wear his own life jacket, though. Not enough flotation in it, they'd said. So it was time to submit to a fitting for an ugly Sam's Adventure Tours life jacket.

As Peter ambled over, he glanced at Neeta in her new wetsuit. Seventeen, huh. Too old but not bad on the eyes. Plus she had a super-nifty camera he'd have to ask her about later. Even nicer than his, he had to admit. He scanned the lineup, trying on life jackets.

"Hey Neeta, do you need help buckling that up?" he tried, to no reply, not that he expected one.

When everything was loaded, each passenger had been outfitted, and everyone had gathered for the safety talk, Peter stood, feet kicking the pebbles in front of him, waiting for the big lecture. Jake pulled some crumpled notes from his life jacket pocket for the umpteenth time that morning and stroked his stomach as if to chase the butterflies away. As Nancy gave him the nod, Jake stepped forward, coughed, and forced a smile at the gathered passengers. Ron, Kate, and Angus, who'd heard it all before, moved to a growing patch of sunlight near the lapping waves. Peter wondered if it would be rude to join them. He watched Vinay move close to the Joshis.

"Welcome to the Cattibone," Jake began, stuffing his notes back into his life jacket pocket and wiping his palms on his wetsuit's thighs. "Welcome to the Cattibone, which runs at a volume of seventeen thousand cubic feet per second. That means it's a big river running medium high, which hopefully means nothing but fun and excitement for the next eight days."

"Alright!" Peter shouted. A few passengers looked at him. Jake shuffled his wetsuit boots on the hard ground.

"Whitewater rivers are rated on a scale of 1 to 5, 1 being something a grandmother can drift down on her inner tube, and 5 being dangerous even to expert boaters. We'll be covering about twenty miles a day. The Cattibone is rated Class 4 to 5. It's, um, one hundred and seventy-five miles of rapids. That includes a ninety-five-mile canyon of whitewater."

"Yes!" Peter whispered, grin cracking his face.

Jake paused, lifted his wrinkled notes from the pocket again and ran a hand over his stomach as he located his place.

"The canyon starts just below a section famous for grizzly bears. Besides grizzlies, we could see black bears, moose, cougars, eagles, kingfishers, gulls, osprey, and lots of other birds that Angus, a dedicated birdwatcher, can tell you about.

"Because of all the, ah, wildlife, we ask that no one take food or dirty dishes into their tents at any time. Each evening, the guides will put all foodstuffs in a bag and hang it between two trees. That's so animals can't reach it."

He tucked his notes away again, refusing to look at Peter, who was trying to make faces at him. Peter was getting bored with this. He noticed that Mrs. Joshi was also looking around and fidgeting. Then he saw Vinay speaking low into her ear. Translating. So that's how he'd gotten on this trip, Peter thought.

"We ask that you check with a guide before going for walks away from the campsite, and that you explore only in groups. On the river …"

Jake looked up. Peter followed his annoyed glance to the dentists, who were whispering among themselves.

"Gentlemen," Nancy intervened for him. "Please listen up, since this information could save your lives."

Jake coughed. "On the river, each paddle captain — that's Kate and Vinay — will explain the commands and basic safety rules as you board this morning. In general, you'll be straddling the tubes with one foot tucked into toeholds on the floor. That's to help keep you from falling out on bouncy sections. In rocky sections, your guide may tell you to pull both legs in. If you fall out of your raft, try to hold onto your paddle. It gives you flotation and helps us pull you back on board. Finally" — Peter watched Jake draw himself up to his full height — "if you find yourself in the river, keep your feet up and pointed downstream until a raft or kayak is able to get to you. This allows you to use your feet, rather than your head, to bounce off rocks. And if one of the kayakers comes to rescue you, grab onto the bow or stern — I mean the front or rear — not the middle. Otherwise, you'll capsize your rescuer.

"Which is sure to lose you your evening beer privileges!" Ron shouted from shore.

"No way!" cried two of the New Zealand dentists, Jim and his brother Derek, as everyone laughed. Everyone but Peter, who was impatient to get on the river. But no, Jake still had a last word.

"Although you've all said you want to paddle in the paddle rafts for now, if anyone decides they need a rest, I would be more than happy to give up my spot in the front of the oar raft. Any questions?"

Not likely, thought Peter, raising his arms with an exuberant cheer and sprinting for Vinay's raft. First in, first choice of seat, he reckoned, and right up front was where he, Peter Montpetit, belonged. He leaped in, paddle in hand, and let loose a wild "Yahoo!"

Soon cheering filled the air as everyone bounded for their boats, paddles in hand. Peter watched with a twinge of jealousy as Ron and Angus climbed into their kayaks. As he looked over at Jake, he recognized the same wistful gaze.

Peter's parents, looking a little uncomfortable in their neoprene suits, and the dentists, all athletic-looking and age thirty at most, climbed into Kate's raft, where she positioned the two strongest, most confident-looking passengers — Jim and Derek — in the front and motioned Laura and Richard Montpetit just forward of her back-rim seat.

Peter smiled. Probably just as well. His parents were pretty cool as parents went but probably not up to front-row splash zones yet. It was their first raft trip, after all. He glanced at his tall, fit dad stepping in like a gentleman, running a finger uncertainly down his gray sideburns.

"Hey, I'm used to piloting," he joked.

"Yeah, but you haven't earned your wings on this craft yet," his mother teased.

Good one, Mom. Peter broke into another yahoo as he bounced on his tube seat, impatient to get going.

Across from him, the kind-looking Dr. Joshi sat down and smiled. Mrs. Joshi, shy but smiling, perched delicately behind her husband. Peter smirked as he spied Vinay prolonging the gentle grip he had on Neeta's arm while helping her into the spot across from her mother. Neeta's shy face gave nothing away as she let go of Vinay's hand, situated herself on the raft's back corner, and tucked her waterproof camera into her life jacket.

"Jake old buddy, so sorry to see you stored like a ship's rat," Peter called out to his friend already in the front of Nancy's boat. Behind him, Nancy sat tall amid carefully balanced stacks of gear bags.

"Yeah, well at least we get to be the first down each rapid," Jake replied.

Peter helped Vinay push their raft away from shore and jumped aboard just as the craft began floating downstream. He watched Jake do the same from Nancy's boat. As he straddled his tube like a cowboy, Peter savored the taste of the cold spray and leaned into it, pretending to be a Viking ship's figurehead.

"Too bad the big rapids don't start until tomorrow," he lamented as Vinay stuck his extra-long paddle into the water to rudder. Soon trees winked by and eddies spun like lazy pinwheels along their peaceful green highway.

"Keep your eye out for pictographs — ancient rock drawings," Nancy called out. Her raft floated around a corner and slipped into a small sandstone cave that appeared in the cliff. Vinay's raft followed suit, which perked Peter up. Kate's raft bumped theirs softly as she and the two kayakers brought up the rear.

Here, water dripped like musical notes that echoed off high arches above. The hushed feel of the place reminded Peter of a chapel. At first, he could see nothing but the varied waterlines that marked centuries of seasonal river tides. Then he followed Nancy's outstretched arm to spot a row of strange ochre figures etched on a ledge overhead. The reflection of flickering waves gave the Indian paintings a magical sense of movement. They seemed to be dancing forward while at the same time peering back at their visitors.

Peter wanted to ask Nancy what they meant and why she was slipping out of the cave before he could focus his camera, but Vinay held a finger to his mouth and breathed, "Shhh." Like there was a rule of silence in there or something.

"But —" Peter protested as they exited the cave. Vinay cut him off. "Disrespectful trespassers have damaged many of these sites. Nancy doesn't always share these with clients. But she believes that studying the pictographs, respecting them, and, above all, protecting them, brings us protection on our trip."

"What?" Peter thought, kicking his tube and tucking his camera away as Vinay repeated the comments in his other language. "That woman *is* a witch." He wasn't about to ask her more about the caves. Still, he couldn't help feeling special just for having glimpsed the ancient markings. Not for the first time, he felt an almost religious reverence for wilderness rivers, which can take a person so easily to places other people can't discover. This peaceful world was so far removed from his Seattle life, with its video arcades and shopping malls and school fights. Peter loved both the tranquility and exuberance of wild rivers. And he wondered if there would be other caves to explore on this trip, other caves with secrets.

6   The Wild West

"Hey, Jake and Nancy!" Peter called out as his raft floated to within shouting distance. "Want to race?"

"Any day!" Nancy tossed back. "Next rapid is Class 2, by the way, so heads up!"

Jake leaned back, tucked his hands behind his head, wriggled his wetsuit boots, which hung over the bow, and smiled as Nancy dipped her oars and worked her glistening shoulders.

"Don't get too relaxed, Jake."

"Um hmm."

"Hard forward," Jake heard Vinay command his team of paddle-wielding customers. Then Vinay stretched his long guide's paddle out to one side to rudder his craft toward the dark V that marked the top of the rapid. Peering over the heads of his passengers to assess the route, he shouted, "Legs in!" as the raft neared a pile of mid-river rocks.

The Joshis and Peter lifted their legs off the tube and tucked them inside safely. But as Jake and Nancy gained on them from behind, Peter slung his leg back over to dig harder into the bouncy waves.

"Not smart, Peter," Jake muttered, knowing before it happened that the next lurch of the raft would sling his impetuous friend into the drink. Splash. Before Vinay could even speak to Peter, Mrs. Joshi stood up and leaned over to lend him a hand.

"Sit down!" Vinay commanded, but it was too late. Over the slippery side went Anita Joshi. She bobbed to the frothy surface with one hand clutched on her paddle, eyes wide, nose flared and mouth gaping.

"Feet up and downstream, and hold onto that paddle," Vinay shouted as he reached to maneuver the raft through the last patch of turbulence. Angus shot over to Mrs. Joshi in his kayak. She grabbed him around the waist.

Over went Angus, leaving Mrs. Joshi flailing for a second until he spun back upright, smiled, and said, "Tail end, please." Soon he'd towed her back to the raft, where many pairs of hands helped her aboard.

As the water drained from her black wetsuit, she beamed. "Good sport, yes?" she said.

Everyone cheered.

"Yes, you are a very good sport," Angus told her, removing his helmet to shake his curls and beard like a poodle who'd stepped in a puddle.

"So, who won, anyway?" Peter demanded.

"Tie. And here's our lunch spot," said Jake as he spied a sandy beach off a clearing in the tall, sweet-smelling trees. Ron and Angus, kayaks turned upstream to play in gentle waves like surfers, were the last to beach and amble up to Jake's makeshift sandwich-making operation. Soon both clients and crew had had their fill, and Jake was repacking the ice chest and dishes sack.

Everyone but Jake was involved in rescue-bag throwing contests, led by Angus. Jake snatched views of the contest between closing up the ice chests, lugging them to the oar raft, and strapping them in place.

"Slave man," he thought. "Oh well, I'm here."

Back on the water a short while later, the rafts slipped by the thickening forest, skirting occasional boulders and riding dinosaur humps of water that rose out of nowhere.

"Yeah! That was fun!" Derek enthused.

Soon, shadows reached like fingers from shore, and Nancy told Jake to help her keep an eye out for a suitable campsite. Jake was the first to spot it: a sun-dappled clearing on the right, with a stream swelled to the top of its banks running through it.

"Perfect!" Jake said. Nancy nodded to him as she shipped her oars. Jake leaped into the shallows to tie their bowline to a tree and waded out further to help secure Kate's and Vinay's rafts.

Soon Jake and a few helpers were unloading the rafts, setting up tents, digging the camp toilet, and gathering wood for the campfire. He'd hardly gotten the fire going and dinner organized when Jake heard angry voices in the forest. Pulling pans off the fire, he ran toward the sound of a scuffle.

"Help!" he heard Vinay howl. Charging into a clearing, Jake threw himself on top of Ron, whose giant hulk had Vinay well pinned as the two exchanged blows.

"Stop it, both of you! Ron, cool it!" Jake managed to grip Ron's wrists until the big man unclenched his fists and rolled off Vinay. Without a word, Ron stood up, smoothed his ponytail and sweat-soaked T-shirt, gave both boys a withering look, and strode off.

Vinay lifted a shaking hand to his bruised cheek. Jake, still panting from his sprint, slumped to a cross-legged position and waited.

"He's mean and hot-headed," Vinay declared, brushing dirt off his khaki shorts and new Sam's Adventure Tours T-shirt.

"And you're only hot-headed." Jake frowned and tossed a stone at a tree. "You're lucky I heard you before Nancy, you twit. So how did David and Goliath come to this?"

"I was minding my own business when Ron said, 'If you lose two passengers on a Class 2 rapid, what are you going to do in the canyon?' I said today's swims were harmless and he should mind his own business. He called me a 'lily-livered trainee' with no right to be on the Cattibone, and I reminded him I was a full guide and selected for the trip. That's when he called me a 'twitchy little Paki' who couldn't paddle Class 4 if my life depended on it, and I punched him."

Jake sighed. How could someone who'd guided in the Amazon be so stupidly racist? But Ron was a hothead who often sought trouble, and Vinay — a junior guide up to a few weeks ago — had his own short fuse.

"Vinay, Ron may be a jerk and a creep with a rotten temper, but he's a first-rate guide, and he, Nancy, Kate, and Angus have all paddled the Cattibone several times. You want to work for Sam and Nancy, you want to get down the Cattibone safely, you have to learn to work with him. Anyway, you're lucky you're not hurt. I'm not going to say anything to Nancy. Just come help me serve supper."

Back at the campfire, Jake and Vinay poured steaming shrimp curry and rice onto tin plates as the clients gathered around, sniffing the air, rubbing their hands together, and jockeying for position. Jake glowed as they returned for second and third helpings of both the curry and the fresh vegetable salad and chocolate cake he and Kate had made.

"So, which chef's school did you attend, mate?" asked Jim. Angus had nicknamed him "Hyper Jim."

"My mother's," Jake replied with a smile.

"And are we going to eat like this all the way down the river?"

"No, the ice chests help us out only the first few days. Then we run out of fresh vegetables. We'll be eating most stuff out of cans and packages by the end of the trip."

"Then we'll eat extra heartily tonight," announced Jim, accepting a glass of wine from Ron. "Tell me, son, what happens if one of our rafts smashes into a rock and punctures?"

"That would deflate one chamber, and we'd kinda limp a bit, but each raft tube has a couple of air chambers, like car tires. So most of the time, we can just back off the rock, paddle to shore, patch and re-inflate it, and carry on."

"Clever," Jim said. "And who lives in the forests around here? Is this region completely wild, or is there the odd village or hunter's shack?"

"The land on the opposite, eastern side of the river is First Nations land for one hundred and twenty-five miles. That's the term used for our indigenous people here in B.C., like your Maori people in New Zealand," Angus replied. "There are a few isolated shacks there, and we may see a First Nations fisherman, but we passed their only community, and the only road or trail between our start and finish points, early this morning. This western side of the river is government-protected forest, with nothing but wildlife and trees between here and the coastal mountains. There aren't even hiking trails to bring us into contact with backpackers."

"So we really are in the wilderness," mused Jim. "But if something happened, I presume we're in radio contact with somewhere?"

"We have two cellphones," said Angus, eyes twinkling. "But that doesn't really change the fact that we're in the last of the Wild West."

"Hmmm. Well, who's going to tell us what lies ahead? When do we get to the big stuff?"

"Tomorrow has a few tricky rapids with big waves in the Gorge of No Return," Nancy began.

"Why is it called the Gorge of No Return?" Richard Montpetit's bass voice broke in.

"Because once we pass through it, we can't hike back to our starting point; we're committed to paddling down the rest of the river. Then another stream feeds into the Cattibone and the volume really picks up. On Day Three, we'll camp just above a spectacular waterfall, which is also the heart of grizzly territory, and on Day Four we'll start into a Class 4 canyon. That's where the river truly kicks up. We'll be in the canyon for three days; then we have two long days of quiet water to reach The Forks. Today was just a warm-up. I promise you won't be bored from now on."

"So, how do we get around the waterfall?" asked Peter. "Or do we get to run over it — kaboom, wheeeee, crash?"

Jake watched Nancy turn toward Peter. "The guides will carry the rafts around the falls, and after everyone has climbed back in, crews have only a few seconds' warm-up before we're in the canyon," she said in a no-nonsense voice.

"Awww, you're no fun," said Peter. "So what's the waterfall like?"

It didn't surprise Jake to see Nancy's face turned dark. "There are sharp rocks just below the surface at the bottom of the falls, followed by a short pool, followed by a narrows leading into the canyon." She lowered her voice so that only Peter and the guides could hear. "Last year, the narrows claimed the lives of two fishermen who fell in below the falls and were dragged downstream. Their bodies are believed to have lodged beneath undercut rocks in the canyon walls."

"So we'll not cast our fishing lines there," finished Angus, looking from Nancy to Peter.

"Angus, can I paddle your kayak tonight?" Peter asked, hands folded neatly in his lap and head cocked.

"As long as you stick to those small waves beside camp, and someone is keeping an eye on you," Angus answered.

"I'll keep an eye on him," Peter's father volunteered. Peter frowned but said nothing.

An hour later, Jake was finishing up dishes and pushing another log onto the evening campfire when Peter dripped past him with a triumphant look on his face.

"Awesome boat, Jake. You should try it — plays like a dream. By the way, I've done my workout for today, which puts me one day up on you, I'm afraid." He paused for effect, smirk spreading. "That dish-suds action just ain't gonna cut it for keeping your biceps pumped, y'know. Tell that witch boss of yours to cut you some slack or I'll wallop you at the World Championships, buddy."

Jake's entire body went rigid. He was about to pummel Peter when he felt Ron's hand on his shoulder. "Come on, kid, let's shred some waves together before dark." And so they did — Ron in his kayak, Jake in Angus's — until, tired but happy, Jake turned the boat to shore just as stars began to appear. Sleep would be no problem tonight. And that was just as well, given that he'd be paddling the Gorge of No Return tomorrow.

7   The Island

When Mrs. Joshi opted to trade places with him the next morning, Jake was delighted to board a paddle raft, especially the one that held Peter and Vinay. He'd forgiven Peter already for his taunt the evening before and was looking forward to the more difficult rapids they'd be encountering today.

"Class 3 today," Vinay reminded his passengers. "I need all of you to be bright and alert!"

"Jake is alert, but he has never been very bright," Peter deadpanned, prompting Jake to sweep a paddle-spray of water at him.

"Hey, it's too early to get wet," Peter protested. Neeta giggled and her father smiled. At the lunchtime stop, after they had ridden half a dozen roller-coaster rapids, Jake spread a red-checkered tablecloth on a long, flat rock and unpacked sandwiches, tortilla chips, and guacamole he had made up that morning. As he did so, he noticed a rocky outcrop hanging out over the river from a cliff just downstream.

"That's the entrance to the Gorge of No Return," said Nancy, following his gaze. "The current picks up quickly around the corner and leads into a major rapid we haven't looked at carefully."

"Why do you need to examine a rapid if you've run this river lots of times before?" asked Larry, making himself a triple-decker sandwich from Jake's buffet.

"Because it changes by the day, never mind the year," Kate replied. "Water levels rise and fall with the weather, and sometimes logs wash in and block a route. In high water, house-sized river boulders can even roll to new places in a rapid."

"But we haven't scouted any other rapids," Patrick said. "Why some and not others?"

"Most minor rapids can be scouted from the boat. It would be unnecessary and too time-consuming to scout all the rapids along the way. Anyway, we know the river, which means we know which rapids we need to scout every time, and which ones we don't. Also, where the riverbanks turn into cliffs, it's impossible to scout; that's where the guide's experience becomes crucial."

Just then, Ron squeezed under the outcrop they'd been studying. "I've had a close look downstream," he reported to Nancy. "There's a logjam on the right at the bottom of the first rapid, but we can easily skirt it on the left."

"Thanks, Ron," Nancy replied, throwing Kate and Vinay a look. The guides, unlike the passengers, knew that logs are a whitewater boater's worst enemy. While rocks can stop or tear a raft, they usually let boats and swimmers bounce off them. Logs, on the other hand, often suck objects beneath them and hold them prisoner in underwater branches. Logs on this river could be twice the length of the group's longest raft and heftier than any of the raft tubes. If a log slipped out of a logjam and came barreling down the river like a freight train, it could easily make lunch meat of a raft sandwiched between it and a boulder. Jake and the guides knew exactly how dangerous logs were, and they knew Nancy's furtive look to be a warning.

Nancy, of course, slalomed through the start of the Gorge without incident, using waves that splashed off the cliff walls to help position herself for watery slots between rocks. Kate, captaining the larger of the two paddle rafts, zigzagged through the rapid following Nancy's line with precision.

"Forward, left turn, stop," she shouted in turn at her excited crew. Like Nancy, she gave the logjam plenty of clearance and was soon parked safely beside her boss.

Vinay's voice as he shouted orders struck Jake as a little high pitched, but the raft stayed on line until a hole caught and spun it, then shoved it toward the logjam. Jake held his breath and dug with his paddle for solid water beneath the frothy top currents as Vinay screamed, "Back paddle!" The raft shuddered and slid away from the logjam, then stuck on a sharp rock whose teeth barely protruded above the confused water. As the raft swung around like a Frisbee on a finger, Vinay lunged forward, grabbed Neeta, pushed her into Peter's lap and leaned far back on his own rear tube. This stopped the raft from catching beneath the feet of the startled girl, but not before Jake heard a ripping sound. As the raft parted from its would-be captor, Jake knew that Vinay had handled a dicey situation well. He also knew that while Vinay and the others were recounting the story over lunch, he'd be busy mending the raft's bottom.

As the day rolled on, Jake found himself relaxing to the rhythms of the trip. Though he, like Peter, could hardly bear to watch Ron and Angus rollick in the rapids of gradually increasing intensity, he was beginning to think Peter was okay again, especially when Peter offered to help him unload the rafts both at the lunch break and evening's destination, so that the two of them could play Frisbee together.

That evening, Ron pulled out a harmonica to serenade those toasting a successful run through the Gorge of No Return.

"There's no going back now, by foot or any other means," Kate announced cheerfully. "It's all downriver from here." Everyone cheered.

"Hey," Jim addressed Angus. "You're the birder, right? I saw that you have an illustrated guide. Mind if I borrow it to go exploring in the woods after dinner?"

"Not at all, if you'll let me join you."

"And I can paddle your kayak again?" Peter asked, placing a hand on Angus's arm. Jake noticed that Peter dared not ask temperamental Ron the same favor.

"No problem. Same rules."

Jake had just finished his chores and was thinking of asking Ron if he could borrow his kayak to join Peter when he heard a blood-curdling scream from downriver. This time, it was not the sound of a couple of bad-tempered guides fighting. The agony and volume of the prolonged cries sent an electric shock through Jake's body. He scrambled to his feet, grabbed the wood-cutting ax, and ran toward the noise, with Vinay and some of the rafters at his heels.

"Someone help! Someone!" came Jim's voice, almost drowned out by terrifying wails that sounded like Angus, further away. As the group rounded a bend, Jim's sheet-white face burst out of the brush and he fell to his knees.

"Help him, help him," he gasped. "Get Dr. Joshi fast or he'll die."

Laura Montpetit sprinted back toward the tents for Dr. Joshi. Jake and his frightened followers ran past Jim toward the unceasing bellows of pain. Jake was the first to reach the beach across from a small island where Angus was kneeling, his face covered with blood, arms outstretched for a handhold as he crawled blindly toward the water's edge. There was no sign of a wild animal; indeed, the island to which Angus and Jim had waded would never have held a bear or moose. Nor was there any sign of a human. Glancing warily into the darkening woods behind them, Jake handed the ax to Vinay.

"Stand guard," he urged as he waded into the hip-deep water to make his way to Angus.

"I'm here," Jake said, taking Angus's outstretched hands and trying not to lose his stomach at the sight of the guide's mangled face. From the first-aid training Nancy had given her guides, Jake knew he must first try to calm Angus. But the big man, thrashing about as if blind and crying in pain, would not be quieted. He pushed Jake's hands away and plunged his bloodied face into the mud, twisting his head back and forth, while covering the back of his head with his arms as if expecting an attack. Jake, racking his brain for what to do, lowered himself to his hands and knees and hugged Angus until the cries became more subdued. Then Jake tore off the shirt he was wearing beneath his wetsuit and dipped it into the river beside him.

He couldn't help hesitating before applying the makeshift sponge. Angus's entire face looked like vicious claws had raked it, Jake thought. As he lowered the wet shirt onto Angus's eyes, the injured guide began shrieking again. Jake wiped sweat from his own forehead and searched Angus's face for an obvious flow of blood but could find none: only a strange, angry blanket of raw punctures and scratches. The man's face looked as though it had been clubbed by a baseball bat and wrapped tightly in barbed wire.

"Angus," Jake whispered, hands cupping the large man's head. "Dr. Joshi is on his way. Just breathe deeply and tell me if anything is hurt besides your face." Angus sobbed and buried his face against Jake's chest, but managed to shake his head no.

"Can you walk across the channel with me if I guide you?" No answer. Then, slowly, Angus nodded.

"I'm here!" Nancy called from across the channel. Jake turned to see his normally calm boss halt, her face drain of all color, and her mouth drop open and hang there. Clutching the raft's first-aid kit to her chest, she leaped into the channel. Together, they wrapped their arms under Angus's armpits and helped him stagger through the channel to the main shore just as Dr. Joshi appeared toting his medical bag. Laura Montpetit followed Dr. Joshi, carrying towels and a sleeping bag.

Laura helped Angus sit on a flat boulder and quickly set to work drying him with the towels before draping the sleeping bag across the victim's shivering shoulders. Flight attendants are trained for emergencies, Jake recalled.

"I — came — as — fast — as …" A panting Kate stopped, surveyed the group for a split second, then placed her hands on Laura's back to lead her away.

"Let's give them some privacy," she urged.

"Vinay," she added as he crashed through the brush with Jim, Derek, Patrick, and Larry on his heels, "lead everyone back to camp and get some tea going, okay? All except Jim." She eyed Jim's trembling body and pasty face and led him to a stump beside Angus. "Maybe you can tell Nancy what happened. The rest of us are out of here."

She shooed Vinay, Laura, and the other three dentists up the path like a mother hen.

Nancy kneeled in front of Angus, took his hands in hers, and turned to Jim. "What happened, Jim?"

"We found a great blue heron — very rare for this region — and saw that she was caught in some fishing line. Angus was trying to free her when she attacked his face with no warning. Her beak was five inches long and sharp like a dagger. She lashed him viciously. I drove her away with sticks, but it was too late. She had gone straight for his eyes."

Dr. Joshi's deft hands removed Angus's eye wrap despite the guide's moans and Nancy's wincing.

"And very nearly eliminated them," he said softly. "The bird has caused penetrating injuries. Angus is suffering from shock, contusions, abrasions, and lacerations, and I suspect a cheekbone fracture." He paused as he met blank stares from Jake, Nancy, and Jim.

"Sorry. He's got bruises, scratches, and cut skin that will swell and cause temporary distorted vision. Still, it's not life threatening and hopefully, he'll regain normal sight within a few days. Luckily, I've got some medical supplies. Let's get him back to camp where I can wash his wounds with cooled boiled water."

Nancy touched Dr. Joshi's arm lightly. "Will he need evacuation or hospitalization?"

"Not likely," Dr. Joshi replied. "I've got everything he could need. He's in good hands. He may even recover fully before we're down the river."

Nancy nodded, her face relaxing a little.

8   The Oar Raft

It was a somber camp that awoke to Day Three of the expedition. Nancy had sat beside Angus in his tent all night, offering him drinks of water, trying to comfort him when he cried out. Jake knew she had also been stewing over a plan. Angus would need to ride in the front of the oar raft now, probably with someone to nurse him there, but Jake wasn't sure what Nancy would do about Angus's kayak.

"I can paddle it down the river," Peter had offered.

"Not likely. Sorry, Peter," Nancy had replied.

Last night, Jake had overheard Nancy telling Ron, "Our insurance would cover Jake paddling the kayak, but I'd rather he sat with Angus. Let me make the decision in the morning, okay?"

Now, as Nancy and Dr. Joshi emerged from Angus's tent after changing his dressings, Nancy — moving slowly and with dark circles under her eyes — motioned to Jake.

"Jake, I may let you paddle the kayak tomorrow, but for today, we're going to lash it to the back of the oar raft, and I'd like you to keep Angus as comfortable as possible in the front of the raft. If I get too tired today, I may need to change places with you. I know you can handle an oar raft."

"Whatever you need," Jake replied. "How is Angus doing?"

"His face is more swollen than yesterday, as Dr. Joshi predicted, but he's no worse. I think he just needs to be kept as quiet and comfortable as possible. He won't eat, but we've coaxed some water into him. Please help downplay the situation to clients."

Jake nodded. The kayak lashed on top of gear in the rear of Nancy's raft resembled a strange pair of wings on a squat body. Jake decided the boat looked like a lumpy flying insect, one unlikely to take off on command. Still, he figured their creaking craft would make it through the day, which involved Class 3½ rapids separated by long, quiet pools, Kate had said. Jake and Nancy piled soft rubber gear bags into a nest for Angus, and though the guide groaned mightily at being moved, he went quiet once in the raft. Once they had pushed off from shore, Jake placed his hands in Angus's to reassure him someone was near, and shaded his head with a camping pad duct-taped to gear bags in a way that wouldn't block Nancy's view.

When the boats stopped for lunch, Nancy offered

to serve while Jake stayed in the raft with Angus. From his perch, Jake watched Peter and Neeta comparing their cameras on the beach and Vinay organizing the rest of the passengers for a rock-skipping contest.

By mid-afternoon, Jake noticed that Nancy looked bleary-eyed. Her worry and lack of sleep had clearly worn her down. "Shall I take a turn at the oars?" he asked. She smiled, nodded, and climbed into the front compartment beside Angus.

The river ambled by scenic woods and occasional spits of sand, at one point braiding into two channels. Jake, junior guide extraordinaire, knew to take the fuller one, of course. The sun, its heat fading as Jake conquered one rapid after another, carried just enough force to chase away goosebumps on his bare arms and turn waves into sparkling champagne.

A few miles from where they were likely to stop for the night, the river picked up, and Jake wondered if he should wake Nancy, who had fallen asleep against Angus's shoulder. A moment's indecision allowed the raft to drift toward a horizon line below which thundered a rapid.

"I'll just keep going," Jake decided. Sitting up as straight as he could, running a hand over his stomach, he surveyed the steep drop from the top of the first wave and mentally drew a line through the maze of rocks. Not too difficult, he judged, just kind of rocky. "Mustn't let my oars catch on a rock or pop off their clips," he reminded himself. Nancy, unlike other guides, never tied a safety line between her oars and oarlocks. She'd once seen a safety line tangle around a passenger when the raft flipped. Although no one had been hurt, the potential disaster had made her mind up about that.

As Jake's raft began to twist through its obstacle course, his heart drummed against his chest. This was more technical than he'd bargained for, and it didn't help that the other rafts were following his lead. As the raft bruised its first rock, Nancy awoke and spun around to look at Jake. He hoped she would not notice his sweaty palms and brow, for it was too late now to change drivers. He was halfway through the rapid, wincing with each soft blow to the rubber sides and trying not to hear Angus's moans, when he noticed a razor-sharp rock waiting for him midstream. Pulling hard to the left, he missed it by a whisker, but when he tried to pull back right, his left oar hit a rock, popped off its oarlock, and flew through the air. The splash announcing the river had just claimed his oar scrambled Jake's brain. He shifted back and forth on his seat, trailing his single oar, and watched the raft bear down on a boulder the size of a barn. What could he do? Leap up and lean into the boulder? As if that would stop a heavy freight raft from wrapping itself around the wall and spilling out all the camp's gear, Nancy, and a helpless Angus.

As he sat dumbstruck, Nancy jumped up and, in one blurred motion, stepped over Angus and unlashed the spare oar from the side of the raft. She heaved it at the boulder like a hunter spearing a whale, pushing her hard body against it as sweat streamed down her brow. The raft slowed and changed course ever so slightly, just enough. The force of her action saved the raft from collapsing but spun it to the downstream edge of the rock, where it hit with sickening force, throwing a shrieking Angus into a heap inside the raft. Then the raft bounced clear.

Without pause, Nancy turned, snapped the spare oar into the empty oarlock, nodded at Jake, and sat down to rearrange Angus. Jake pulled once again, astonished that Nancy had not fallen into the water between the raft and rock, or dropped her heavy spear as she leaned all her weight into it.

"She just risked her life to push the raft away," he thought, "and I, Jake Evans, just blew it big-time. I'm a complete failure." Why hadn't he thought of the spare oar, or used his remaining one to push them away like Nancy had? Hot anger at himself for bringing them within a hair of disaster put new power into his tugs on the oars. He picked his way through the rest of the maze with all the determination he'd applied to slaloming through the gates at team trials. But his new show of confidence melted when he reached an eddy at the bottom. He hung his head, unable to look at Nancy.

"It's okay," she said as she rose to change places with him. "All's well that ends well. Now help me pad Angus again." Their efforts were interrupted by a shout from upstream.

"Like my new paddle?" Ron called out as he appeared from behind the same barn-sized boulder that had nearly done in Jake's boat. Jake's jaw lowered. The trip's ponytailed, bare-shouldered muscleman was twisting his way through the rock garden using the lost oar like a kayak paddle. Never mind that it was nine feet long, had a blade at only one end, and weighed nearly as much as his kayak. Only Ron could have snaked in and out of the rocks like that, even pausing to clown on a wave. Drawing up at last to the waiting rafts, he asked casually, "Has anyone seen my other paddle?"

Vinay, sitting in an eddy nearby, smiled as he dived to the bottom of his raft to toss the paddle to Ron.

Nancy leaned down and slapped Ron on the back. "Would've taken us hours to find that in the rock garden, and we'd have cut our legs up trying," she said. "Or we'd have had to spend our entire season's beer money to replace it. What a man, Ron."

"At your service, ma'am." And he executed three perfect cartwheels in his kayak — flipping end to end, kayak and all — ponytail flying.

"Ron's happy," Jake translated, reminding himself to tap Ron for cartwheel lessons sometime during the trip.

They made camp early that evening, on a beach a mile upstream from where Nancy said the thirty-foot vertical falls was located. Jake took care to pitch Angus's tent further from the campfire than usual to give him some peace, then moved a distance away to hang the line that would hold the food bags at bedtime.

"Nancy, permission please to hike down and see this reputedly magnificent falls," Jim asked, his three buddies, all with matching hiking boots, pressed close behind him.

Nancy, who'd slumped down outside Angus's tent with a cap pulled low over her face, raised her deep-set eyes and looked at Jim. "Sorry, what did you ask?"

"Permission to hike to the falls before supper?"

Nancy shifted her eyes to Jim, Derek, Larry, and Patrick, as if seeing them for the first time.

"Sure. Just stay together and make some noise on the trail. For bears, I mean." She managed to smile, then pulled the cap lower and resumed staring at the ground.

Jake tiptoed past her to enter Angus's tent with the pot of freshly boiled water Dr. Joshi had requested. "Anything else I can do to help?" he whispered, backing toward the tent door as Dr. Joshi removed the old bandage and Angus's arms began flailing.

The disfigured face grossed him out.

Dr. Joshi smiled at Jake, placed two fingers on Angus's wrist and said, "Know how to take a person's pulse?"

"Uh-huh," Jake said, backing away a little farther.

"Perhaps you could place that thermometer in his mouth for me." When doing so made Angus cry out, Jake mumbled "sorry" and flew out of the tent, never so anxious to begin supper duties.

At supper, Kate eyed Nancy and moved to sit between her and Jake.

"Have an early night, Nance. I'll look after Angus, and Ron will take charge of the camp."

"Are you sure?" Nancy said, her voice hardly more than a whisper.

"Go," Kate urged, giving her a quick hug.

After supper, Ron ambled over to Jake as he was drying dishes. "Hey kid, you're taking this slave thing far too seriously. Sit down and have a beer."

Jake peered at him and shook his head as Ron reached into the beer and wine box reserved strictly for clients.

"Suit yourself, kid." Before the lid of the box slammed back into place, Jake frowned. How could the New Zealanders have finished off half the night's supply of alcohol already?

Ron peeled back the metal tab with practiced hands, sank into a folding chair, and took a few deep swigs. "Angus ain't so good, eh, kid? But he'll be okay. We just gotta keep our minds off things and keep the clients happy. Happy clients pay our board 'n' keep."

He tilted his head back to drain the can, then looked past Jake to the party of hikers returning from the falls.

"Happy clients," he repeated, crushing the can in his powerful hand and hiding it behind the camp chair.

"Well worth the hike!" Jim announced, breathing hard from the climb. "It's a tall one, and straight down."

"Ron," Peter addressed the guide, "Neeta and I want to hike back once more for photos. Is that okay with you?"

"Go for it, boy. And make 'em pretty."

Peter gave Neeta a high-five and pulled her away. Jake noted that his tent mate took off without even a glance in Jake's direction. Well, at least Peter was keeping busy and happy, which took the pressure off Jake when he had to work.

"Jake, my man," Ron said. "The happy clients appear to be absorbed in a game of badminton. What say you we put Vinay in charge and go surf some waves?"

"You bet!" Jake said, sprinting to his tent to don his wetsuit.

Ten minutes later, Jake arrived ahead of Ron on the

shore beside the tethered rafts. He climbed into Angus's kayak and looked around for Ron's kayak, chuckling when he realized Ron had probably hidden it in the bushes from Peter. As Ron appeared, Jake fixed the sprayskirt in place, strapped on his helmet, and moved onto a gentle play wave.

"Where's my kayak?" Ron suddenly roared. "That rat has taken it without my permission!"

Jake, startled, turned and looked at Ron, who returned his gaze meaningfully. Both glanced downstream, squinting into the shadows, hoping, fearing, beginning to panic.

"Damn him! He's planning to go over the falls! In *my* kayak," Ron bellowed, hurtling the helmet he had in his hand into the bottom of the oar raft. "Let's go get him!" Ron ripped the raft's tether from its moorings and leaped into the boat, pointing it downstream in the meanest temper Jake had ever seen.

"Come on!" he ordered in a voice that made Jake sprint his kayak fearfully after the raft. Within moments, they could hear the thunder of the falls and taste the spray that crept upstream from its edge. Still there was no sign of Peter. Jake paddled frantically for shore as he began to fear that Ron, full of rage and beer, was not acting sensibly. On the right side of the river, he spotted two final eddies, the last two places the boats could safely reach without danger of being pulled over the falls. With a bolt of adrenaline, Jake stroked for the first one, shouting at Ron to do the same. He could see Ron pulling backwards on his oars, expertly swinging the boat around to head into the last eddy. Ron had plenty of time to make it and Jake was relieved that Ron had no intention, after all, of dropping over the falls. But as Jake swung into his chosen eddy, he felt hot waves of horror wash over him. A log the size of a flatbed truck was barreling down on Ron.

"Watch out, Ron!" he screamed, his words drowned out by the roar of the falls. Ron's raft was still forty feet from the lip of the falls, and only half that from the last eddy. His enormous arm muscles flexed and bunched as sweat poured down his neck. But as he angled the raft in for a landing, he still hadn't seen the log behind him.

If anyone can make it, Ron can, Jake thought. But that's not the way it turned out. Unable to look away, Jake was forced to witness Ron turn and catch his first and last glimpse of the log, which crashed into the raft with such force it skidded like a hovercraft toward the thundering horizon line. Jake watched Ron drop the oars and reach out toward him as both raft and log performed a slow, sickly arch over the edge of the falls.

9   Peter's Story

Jake wanted this to be part of a nightmare, wanted desperately to pinch himself and wake up. But as he sat in his kayak clinging to tree roots and shivering in the gathering gloom, he knew he must climb out and look over the precipice. He expected to see two bodies below: Ron's and Peter's, and whatever was left of their boats. He wondered whether he could scramble down the bank and reach someone still alive, rescue them, pull them ashore. Not because he wanted to be a hero, not even after blowing things earlier. He just couldn't bear to lose two friends — yes, Peter was still his friend, he knew that now. He didn't want to witness the results of two waterfall-jumping accidents. The Cattibone was strong. The Cattibone was beautiful and wild. But why should she be so cruel, so brutal, all in one trip?

Battling numb and uncooperative legs, Jake pulled himself out of the kayak and tugged it up the bank.

With feet that felt like rocks, he moved forward, both drawn to and repelled by the force of the water pounding over the ledge. He stuck his hands over his ears to block out the din and wiped a hand across his face as the murky clouds of spray washed it. Crawling as close as he dared, he watched thin, glassy sheets of water shatter as they hit sharp rocks beneath the pool's surface thirty feet below. He could see one clear spot, one tongue between stone fangs, a dark green path enveloped by mist. It was wide enough to catch a well-aimed kayaker, maybe, but too narrow to spare even a lucky rubber raft from a direct hit on the rocks. Shielding his eyes from the cold sauna, Jake could make out a calm stretch following the fall's base. It was a stretch he'd have considered attractive on any day other than today. But even that pool was short-lived. A stone's throw from the falls, the river curled into a serpent and writhed headlong into a narrows. The constricted entryway was marked by dark, sculpted walls with no view around the corner — no handhold, no toehold, no view or way in, except by boat.

He remembered Nancy's words of only a day ago: "There are sharp rocks just below the surface, fol-lowed by a short pool, followed by a narrows leading into the canyon. Last year, the narrows claimed the lives of two fishermen who fell in below the falls and were dragged downstream. Their bodies are believed to have lodged beneath undercut rocks in the canyon walls." To enter the narrows, Jake knew, was to commit to many miles of heavy whitewater.

As the evening light dimmed, Jake's eyes scanned the riverbank between the falls and the tunnel-like canyon entrance for any sign of life, any debris. That's when he spotted Peter and Neeta scrambling up rocks beside the entrance to the canyon. Peter was alive! Alive! Jake felt crazed with relief, frantic with excitement. He wanted to hurl himself down the steep slope to hug his buddy. Then he remembered Ron and realized that Peter must have seen him, might have rescued him, might even need Jake's help rescuing him right now. Before bolting down the steep slope, Jake scanned the scene quickly again. Where was the oar raft? And where was the kayak?

He backed away from the edge of the cliff and searched for the best way down. Soon he was scrambling, sometimes tumbling, through thorny bushes that tore at his wetsuit. Who cared? Peter was alive and maybe Ron was too. He only knew he had to get down there, had to help Peter pull Ron to safety. He slid in an avalanche of dirt the last little way and continued on toward Peter and Neeta, leaping over rocks, pushing tree branches out of his way, stumbling and picking himself up again. Once, catapulting between two boulders, he landed on top of Peter's kayak — make that Ron's kayak. The momentary surprise only spurred him to run faster, out of the spray and ear-piercing clamor of the waterfall and toward the mist and evil rumble of the dark canyon.

"Peter! Neeta!" he shouted, sprawling forward and grabbing at their legs, dragging them back from the craggy entrance and hugging a surprised Peter. "What are you doing? Where's Ron? What happened?"

Peter, instead of replying, turned to Neeta. Jake read the answer in her reddened eyes even before she spoke. "He never surfaced," she said. "He never came up. I watched the whole time."

Jake, too numb to think, allowed Neeta and Peter to lead him to a safe point on shore. There, Neeta lowered herself to a cross-legged position and scanned the river in an endless, back-and-forth motion, tears splashing on the smooth pebbles around her.

Peter led Jake a short way further upstream and collapsed against a rock. He lifted his eyes quickly and saw Jake waiting, motionless.

"I talked Neeta into standing at the bottom with a camera and rescue rope," he said, his voice a heavy monotone. He just couldn't summon the energy to speak any way else. "She thought it was all harmless fun. I convinced her that we do vertical falls like this all the time. I'd figured out where to go, my exact line, and I knew how to make sure I landed in the clear channel, the safe spot. I spent lots of time working it out, Jake; I don't care what you say. Anyway, I figured that Neeta was there at the bottom with the rescue rope if things went wrong. So after she decided where to stand with the camera, I left her, hiked back to camp, borrowed Ron's boat and ran the falls. I landed right where I wanted to, and Neeta got the photo."

Jake said nothing, but the look on his face communicated plenty. Peter wasn't sure he could continue with his story if Jake kept glaring at him like that. "Stop," he said. "Stop giving me that look."

Peter stared down at his feet. "Anyway, I had just paddled to shore to thank her when I saw her look up and scream. I never saw Ron. I only heard a terrific crash and saw the raft upside-down in the current with the log rolling off it. What a mother of a log. I thought the raft was empty. I figured its rope had come loose and it had drifted down to the falls. My only thought was to try and retrieve it. So I handed one end of the rescue rope to Neeta and told her to tie it around a tree. While she was doing that, I jumped into the water with the other end and waited until the log floated by. Then I swam to the raft. It was still upside-down, of course, and floating toward that slot into the canyon. I tied my rope to it and swam back to help Neeta pull it in. She was yelling at me, but I couldn't hear what she was saying. The rope was tightening between the little tree she'd tied it to and the raft, and then there was this loud crack. The tree she'd chosen was dead and hollow, and it broke and flew at her, knocking her down. The raft pulled the tree into the river just as I came out of the water. I saw Neeta kneeling on the beach crying, and I saw the raft heading toward the slot. I had two seconds to decide between helping Neeta, who I thought was hurt, and jumping into my kayak to chase what *I* thought was an empty raft. I went back to Neeta, of course. Turns out she was just bruised and scared, but she kept saying, 'Ron, Ron.' I turned and looked back at the falls, and that's when I saw Ron's helmet on the rocks. I take it he never put it on?"

Peter's voice broke. He stopped, squeezed his eyes shut, and pulled his shaking hands into his lap. He felt as if all the blood had drained from his face; he was cold and shaky. But he knew he had to continue.

"There was no sign of Ron at the base of the falls. I dove in and swam to the tongue and kept diving down, but it was no use. Nothing there. So Neeta and I climbed up those rocks near the slot to try and see the canyon, in case the raft or Ron had hung up somewhere we could get to. That's when you got here." He paused, head hung low. "It must be well into the canyon by now, and it's dark."

He could feel the tears welling in his throat and then in his eyes. He couldn't keep them there and they spilled on to his cheeks, warm and stinging. "Why, Jake? Why did Ron run the waterfall in the raft? It's too high for a raft, and the slot is too narrow."

"He was chasing you, Peter. He saw you'd taken his kayak and he wanted to stop you before you reached the falls. The log pushed him over the edge as he was trying to catch an eddy above the falls."

Peter covered his face with his hands and stayed that way even when Neeta moved over and rested her hand on his shoulder.

Jake thought about comforting Peter, but lava deep within him was heading toward eruption. He rose and backed away. Neeta lifted her wet lashes. Her eyes searched Jake's hardening face.

The darkness that had descended on them seemed to be full of hands pulling at Jake from all angles. He stood there, shaken by anger, confusion, indecision, and panic until an invisible hand shoved him toward the falls. Without pausing, Jake threw his life jacket onto the beach and dived in. With sure, steady strokes, he reached the green tongue, the only place a falling body would have had a chance of surviving. Down he plunged into the inky blackness, as far as his wetsuit and his lungs would let him go. Arms flailing, he searched, however stupidly, for anything other than sharp rocks that tore his hands. Again and again he surfaced and dived, blinded by the spray and the dark. He even wriggled, seal-like, up onto one jagged tooth beside the small pool and threw his arms around a large, loose boulder, which he managed to wrestle to the edge of the rock platform. Then he rolled off clutching it in his arms and held on tightly as it took him deeper than he could ever have gone on his own. As soon as he released it, he extended both arms out as far as they could reach, to touch, feel, search every small cavity in the underwater rock cliffs as he kicked slowly to the surface.

Finally, blue with cold and exhaustion, he swam back to shore, where Peter and Neeta, just shadows in the heavy dusk now, stood watching him.

He shook himself off, grabbed his life jacket, and spoke only to Neeta. "Come back to camp with me if you want. Or stay with Peter. I don't care."

And without waiting for a reply, he fled up the hill, pounding his fists into it and yanking viciously at roots, as if that was the only way to create hand- and footholds.

When he reached the top of the rise, Jake felt around for Angus's kayak and kicked it hard before leaning down to hoist it on his shoulder and march back to camp.

As he drew near, he couldn't dodge Vinay, who was starting down the path with a flashlight.

"Jake, are you okay? Where have you been? I thought you and Ron were kayaking by the beach." Vinay stopped and shone his flashlight right on Jake's face.

Jake raised his hand to wave the light out of his eyes. He didn't mean to knock the flashlight to the ground or leave a stunned Vinay standing there. He strode on hollow legs to Nancy's tent, turning briefly when he heard Vinay say, "Neeta?" and saw Neeta throw herself into Vinay's arms.

"Nancy's sleeping." Kate's warning, issued with crossed arms, came from behind him as he hovered in front of Nancy's tent. Slowly, she lowered her arms. "Jake, what is it? Jake? Jake?"

10   Night of Nightmares

That night, the nightmare began almost as soon as Jake's head hit the pillow. He was back in the cave with the pictographs, but it was pitch dark, and he and Nancy were shining their flashlights around the ledges to find the ancient markings. Gradually, the calm water of the cave began circling around them, slow and menacing, then faster and faster until it formed a whirlpool. Jake was in the oarsman's seat. As the raft swirled closer to the center of the whirlpool, Jake pulled frantically on the oars to back away. When one oar flew out of his hand, he slashed at the water helplessly with the other, all the while drawing closer to the deathly grasp of the middle, like a fly caught in water going down a bathtub drain. Nancy just stared at him in a haunting manner, as if resigned to his incompetence.

Then, an eerie green light began to illuminate the dark cave, and the whirlpool's eye widened, growing larger and blacker, hollowing into a cylinder — an empty, dark drop into nothingness. Jake watched, terror-stricken, as a white transparent figure rose in slow motion from the inky middle of the cyclone. It was a ghostly likeness of Ron. As Ron reached the top of the whirlpool, he swiveled slowly to look at Jake — with a sad, blank look. Then he lifted a white-robed arm and handed Jake an oar. Jake, unable to take his eyes off the apparition, clipped the oar in place with numb hands and began to row. He pulled like never before. Slowly, the cyclone's fury eased, the rotations melted into a slow twirl, the green light faded, and Jake was able to muscle the boat back from the brink.

Nancy, who had neither moved nor said anything, now lifted her flashlight to the cave's upper walls and located the colored paintings. This time, both Jake and Nancy could see what the figures represented: three men, a bird, and a wave. As they stared, one of the men turned into a bear that moved like a shadow against the wall. At first, the bear danced in the moonlight reflecting off the gentle motion of the water in the cave. But as Jake watched, the bear grew larger and more sinister, until he leaped off the ledge and began to pad along the surface of the water toward them. Water splashed beneath his massive paws.

Jake gripped the wooden oars so tightly slivers slid into his skin. He wanted to scream and dive into the water but was afraid this would only excite the approaching beast. As Jake and Nancy shrank back, the bear raised a giant paw and sunk it into the tube of the oar raft, slashing the full length of it. The sound of ripping rubber, the hiss of air escaping from the wounded raft, and the bear's agitated growling all rang in Jake's ears as he tried to stifle a scream.

"What more can happen? What more? What more? What more?" he heard Nancy shouting.

Jake awoke in a cold sweat and a high state of alert. He lay very still, trying to draw himself out of the dream and into reality. He was sure something had woken him, but as he lay trembling in his sleeping bag, with ears strained, he could hear nothing. The eerie shadows of moonlit trees danced on the tent ceiling. It was only a nightmare.

He turned over in his sleeping bag and saw Peter lying beside him, fast asleep. Peter hadn't returned to the tent by the time Jake had crawled into bed. He'd probably been helping direct the search party that had hiked down with flashlights and spent another hour searching for Ron's body. Jake, fully awake now, tried to remember the painful conversation with Nancy and Kate the evening before. Something about doing a further search of the waterfall's base and pool in the morning. Something about the expedition's two cellphones being in the raft that went over the waterfall. One had been in a waterproof sack lashed in the raft. The other Ron had taken from Nancy's tent, presumably to phone his girlfriend.

"I saw him put it in his paddling jacket pocket before he headed to the beach," Jim had reported.

Jake remembered Nancy mumbling, through tears, "What more can happen? What more?"

He was afraid of falling asleep again in case the dream returned, so Jake rolled onto his back and studied the shadowy peak of his small tent until his need to empty his bladder grew urgent. He slid out of his bag, trying not to wake Peter, pulled on a fleece jacket against the cool night air, and stuck his feet out the tent door. He stepped into his sneakers and glanced around camp. Not a sound anywhere.

Tiptoeing so he wouldn't wake anyone, he moved to the edge of the clearing and completed his task. As he turned around, he felt, more than saw, a bulky shadow in the moonlight at the other end of camp, then heard strange grunting sounds. Angus making noises in his sleep, he hoped. But when the shadow moved directly into the moonlight, Jake gasped. A bear was wandering through camp, and not a soul knew it but him. Jake stood motionless, the terror of his nightmare returning. Was the beast a small grizzly or large black bear? He knew from years of campfire stories that his safety hinged on getting it right. If it was a grizzly, he'd scramble up the nearest tree. Grizzlies can't climb trees. If it was a black bear, he'd have to play dead and pray, no matter how it knocked him about. Bears, they say, will not eat what they think is a carcass.

The bear, he noted with a shiver, was making the same grunting, snuffling noises as the bear in his dream. He stole a peek at the rafts and drew in his breath. The large paddle raft was shredded along one side — wrecked beyond repair. So the noise had been real. The bear had attacked a raft, and that was what had woken him. Even as the pounding of his heart rose to a deafening volume, Jake wondered why on earth a bear would attack a raft. Bears rarely visit campsites unless food is left lying around. Still frozen in hopes the bear wouldn't notice him, Jake shifted his eyes to the food bag he and Vinay had strung between two trees. It swung softly in the breeze, undisturbed. At least he'd done that job right.

Jake's spine went cold as the beast moved to the center of the campsite and rose on its powerful back legs, sniffing. Thick folds of yellow fur hung around its heavy neck. That made it a grizzly for sure — the most ferocious and unpredictable bear in North America. As its six hundred pounds lumbered in his direction, Jake nearly soiled his thermals. No point playing statue anymore. He chose a tree and leaped to its lower branches. Up, up he climbed, grabbing for higher limbs, moving as fast as his shaking legs would let him. The grizzly moved just as fast in Jake's direction. It halted under Jake's tree and growled softly.

Jake was trembling so hard he was sure he'd lose his grip. He prayed no one would wake up and come stumbling out of their tent. At least he had a chance up here.

"Shhh," he told his attacker through chattering teeth. In answer, the bear rose on its hind legs and reached its forearm straight up the tree. Its outstretched claws stopped only inches below Jake's flailing legs. Sweat poured down his face and his stomach flipped over.

"I need more height," he heard his own pinched voice whisper. He lifted his feet to his abdomen and crawled up into the tree's leafy top. The branches felt thin and unsteady, and he dared not go any further. The bear wasn't impressed. With louder grunts, it pawed the tree, making it sway to and fro. Jake clung tightly to his swinging perch. *I want off this carnival ride.* In seconds, he'd fall out for that bear to scoop up like a hard-won apple.

"Down boy, down." He gulped, hugging the tree with every ounce of strength he had. The bear pushed the small tree even harder and its upper branches brushed against those of the tree beside it. Jake, wide-eyed, caught hold of the other treetop and held on for dear life, forming a tenuous arch that halted the swaying. Teeth chattering but brain still working, he used one arm to whip off his jacket and wrap it around the two thin treetops, then zipped up the jacket hoping that would hold the makeshift pinnacle.

Cowering in the treetop, certain he'd plunge to a hideous death any moment, Jake dared not open his eyes. After a few more shoves, the bear dropped down on all fours and whined. Jake peered down.

"Go away!" he whispered, fighting an urge to cry. To his surprise, the grizzly turned on its heel and ambled into the woods. Jake stayed where he was for a very long time, not daring to unzip the warm jacket he'd have loved to put on. He was half-asleep in his uncomfortable roost when he was woken by incoherent mumbling from Angus's tent and the sound of Kate's footsteps heading for the camp's water jug. The campsite, fully lit by the moon, revealed no sign of a bear. Kate jumped as Jake dropped out of the tree in front of her.

"Jake, you madman. What were you doing up there? Wait, don't tell me; I don't want to know. Can you please fetch Sunil while I boil some water? Angus has taken a turn for the worse."

Jake, too keyed up to return to his own tent after he'd roused Dr. Joshi, followed Kate into Angus's tent and sat in a corner. As Dr. Joshi changed Angus's dressing, Jake forced himself to look at Angus's swollen face. The bruises had turned dark blue and yellow, and Angus, glistening with sweat, called out each time Dr. Joshi touched the swollen patches. The sores smelled awful. Jake felt like a fool for needing to turn away. No way I'm going to be a doctor, he thought.

"He's not responding despite our best efforts," Dr. Joshi was saying to Kate. "Vomiting, nausea, clammy skin, hot and cold spells." He clucked his tongue and shook his head. "Not enough of the antibiotics are getting into him now that he's started vomiting them up." The doctor leaned back on his heels and pressed two knuckles into his cheeks. "The infection has only just now turned bad." His soft hazel eyes rose to meet Jake's and he stretched his arm out to place it reassuringly on Jake's shoulder. "He needs antibiotics intravenously. That means he needs drugs that go through a needle and tube in his arm. This can be done only in a hospital."

The knuckles returned to his face.

"Could he die?" Kate asked.

"There's a remote chance of that," Dr. Joshi replied, his eyes holding Kate's. "But if he starts keeping medicine down and we can get him to a hospital in a few days, he'll pull through. No cellphones now, right? How fast can we get down the rest of the river?"

"Technically, we have five more days, but that's at a leisurely pace," Kate responded. "If we went at top speed, dawn until dusk, we could cut at least one day off, but if we send the kayaks down alone, we might be able to get a helicopter here within three days. Kayaks go faster than rafts."

"That sounds good, but who is going to kayak if both Ron and Angus are — " Dr. Joshi stopped. Kate turned to Jake, who jumped up.

"Peter and I are in top shape. We can do a marathon paddle. We can handle the rapids in the canyon. It's the only way, Kate. Nancy will agree. Besides, I have to tell you something about one of the paddle rafts —"

"What about hiking out?" Dr. Joshi interrupted. "Those dentists are very keen trekkers. What if we pointed them in the right direction? Couldn't they reach help?"

Kate thought for a moment, then looked at Dr. Joshi and Jake in turn. "We'll have to talk this over with Nancy in the morning, but if I ferried the New Zealand guys by raft to the east shore of the river, and they bushwhacked their way due east with a compass, they'd eventually hit the highway the other side of the Cattibone Indian Reserve. It would be slow, rough going, because there aren't any trails, and they'd be trespassing and risking encounters with bears and moose. If we send a hiking and kayaking party at the same time, I think the kayakers will reach help first, but if either runs into trouble, the other party serves as a crucial backup. We can outfit both parties with food from camp supplies — though once the boys' sleeping bags are packed, the kayaks won't hold much — and we'll still have plenty left for ourselves. And we have trip maps for both."

"There's one problem," Jake broke in. "If Peter and I arrive at The Forks two days before we're expected, will the Reserve shuttle drivers have dropped the bus there already? And even if it's there, how are we going to drive it? Neither of us has a driver's license. I've driven a tractor on my uncle's farm, but — "

"We'll take a chance on the bus being there. You'll have a several-day jog if it's not — or, more likely, some vehicle will eventually come down that road and pull over for you. As for driving, this is an emergency, and to tell you the truth, there's not a lot of difference between a tractor in a field and a bus on a deserted gravel road. Anyway, we have no choice."

11   The Canyon

The next morning, after Nancy had gotten over the shock of the damaged raft — which she agreed could not be patched — Derek sheepishly admitted to hijacking a tuna sandwich from their picnic lunch the day before and hiding it in the raft's forward pocket for a mid-afternoon snack. He'd forgotten all about it, but that sandwich was all a grizzly had needed to find their camp and slash the raft.

Nancy and Vinay conducted another search at the waterfall for Ron's body. It had, they concluded, been swept down the canyon under the raft, or was stuck in an underwater crevice unreachable without diving equipment. Nancy approved Kate's plan. Nancy, Kate, Vinay, Angus, the older Montpetits and the Joshis would stay at camp while Jim, Derek, Patrick, and Larry would hike out after being ferried across the river by Kate in the last remaining raft. Peter and Jake packed the two kayaks as Kate prepared food and first-aid kits for both parties.

A solemn crowd gathered on shore to wave good-bye to the New Zealanders. Before stepping in the raft, Kate insisted on hugging Jake and Peter, who rolled their eyes but smiled. The boys also tolerated handshakes all around.

"Stay safe, young man. We love you," Laura whispered as she embraced Peter with watery eyes.

"We're proud of you, son," Richard added, forcing yet another hug on his squirming boy.

"If you see the raft or body snagged somewhere, secure them and mark the location on the map," Nancy instructed Jake with somber eyes. She squeezed his arm fondly and gave him a pleading look. "Be careful, Jake. We're all relying on you." Then she turned away so he could not see the moistness in her dark eyes.

Jake ventured into Angus's tent and knelt, resting his arm on his.

"Is that Jake?" Angus asked in a husky whisper from beneath his bandages.

Relieved to find the big man conscious, Jake squeezed his hand. "How did you know?"

"You're still working on growing hair on your arms."

"I came to say good-bye, Angus. You're going to be alright, you know."

"Be fast and clean," responded the weakened voice. "And trust yourself for reading the currents." He paused, then added, "Trust Peter, too. There's more thoughtfulness to him than he lets on, Jake; he'll help you through." Jake stiffened at that comment and chose not to reply.

Vinay and Neeta helped the boys hike their heavily packed kayaks down to the falls. They set them down on the beach just upstream of the canyon entry, which looked less frightening washed in warm sunlight.

"This will be good training for Nationals," Vinay teased his friend, as if a lighthearted comment could dispel the trauma all four still felt.

"Yeah, and watch that the dish suds don't give you wrinkled hands," Jake shot back half-heartedly. Jake's last glimpse of his send-off party was Neeta poised on a rock behind a tearful Vinay, her chin resting on his head, her beautiful, sad eyes watching them. She was giving Vinay a neck massage.

The canyon, as both Nancy and the map had predicted, offered no warm-up. The minute the boys passed through the craggy slot, giant waves ricocheting off the curved walls pushed and shoved them. Dodging a few rocks, breathing hard, they kept near one another, like football receivers heading for a touchdown.

Jake worried about the extra weight in their boats. They needed time to get used to the unfamiliar load. Not that they'd been able to pack much — just their sleeping bags, mats, rescue ropes, two flashlights, minimal first-aid gear, emergency rations of food, thermal underwear, and water purification tablets. This, Jake figured, doubled the weight of their boats, which made for a major drag on their muscles in slow sections, and a pain in the butt when they tried for fast moves in rapids.

Hey, we're paddling big whitewater and we have sweet kayaks for it, he tried to cheer himself up. But his spirits continued to sag. "Grim" was the only word he could think of to describe the circumstances prompting this desperate rescue mission.

We think we're so hot, but we're just two kids and ninety-five miles of scary rapids, he admitted — in stupidly heavy boats that we have to paddle an impossible number of hours every day till we get there. Thanks to Peter wanting his picture in a magazine, we've lost Ron, a raft, and the cellphones that could have brought rescue helicopters to Angus today. Jake slashed the water harder with his paddle, pulled ahead of Peter and spit at a passing boulder. Then he slowed and sighed. He and Peter had to stick together and select the safest, most conservative lines, what paddlers call "chicken routes." And if either of them capsized, they'd better roll, because taking a swim in challenging whitewater with only one rescuer would be dicey. One lost paddle or boat, and the other would be forced to paddle on alone. And that terrified Jake more than anything that had gone down so far.

He stopped at an eddy as the two approached a steep rapid.

"Gotta read this one on the fly," Peter suggested, pulling into Jake's eddy and placing a hand on Jake's boat to steady the two of them. "The canyon walls won't let us scout, and the eddies all look to be surging."

Jake nodded as he pulled Nancy's waterproof map out of his life jacket pocket. "Looks sketchy, but the map rates it less than a full Class 4. Guess we'll have to trust that." Then, steeled by what he knew to be an unreasonable desire to get away from Peter, Jake peeled out of the eddy and headed down first, without so much as a "good luck."

Every decision on which line to take, Jake had to make from the top of a wave a split second before being hurtled into a trough that blocked upcoming holes and boulders from view. Even with adrenaline pumping through his veins, Jake was fuming at his partner. In return for sneaking around behind everyone's backs, stealing a kayak, and using Neeta, what was Peter getting? Exactly what he'd wanted from the start: a kayak trip down the Cattibone. Did he get what he'd done to Sam's Adventure Tours? Five passengers and four guides were stranded, one needing medical help. Four passengers were forced to turn their raft trip into a hike. Everyone would want their money back, and it would take years for Sam to recover. Never mind Ron's death and two rafts gone, even if one of those hadn't been Peter's fault.

So what if Peter had apologized to Nancy, again and again? Jake couldn't forgive his friend — his former friend. All the relief he'd felt yesterday when he realized Peter was alive had evaporated. If the Cattibone weren't so treacherous, he'd do it solo to get away from Peter. Jake sighed again as he whipped around yet another rock. No he wouldn't. He wasn't *that* stupid.

The sun beat down hard as Jake paused at the bottom of the steep rapid and watched Peter negotiate it like a practiced dancer. Whatever else he was, Peter was a damned good paddler. "I have to stop being mad," Jake told himself. "We're like mountaineers roped together." But when Peter slipped into his eddy with an enthusiastic, "*Nice* one! A *blast*," Jake avoided his eyes and took off again.

Rapid by rapid, they descended the river, keeping their eyes peeled for landmarks such as streams spilling into the Cattibone that confirmed their position on the map. Resisting the urge to play in the waves pained Jake, and so did never letting up on their pace. But at least their race training put them up to it, and the weather was nice. When the sun had been beating down from directly overhead for some time, Jake felt hunger pains begin to gnaw. They had brought very little food with them, and no stove for cooking — there simply wasn't room — but he knew they had to keep up their energy. So, when he spotted a gravel beach between rapids, he motioned to Peter. Peter gave him a thumb's up. They lifted their boats onto the bed of rocks and pulled out two sandwiches.

"At least you've been relieved of lunch-making duties," Peter commented.

"Mmm."

"No sign of the raft yet — I've been looking," Peter tried again.

"Not yet."

"It's hot as Hades today," Peter said, rolling down his wetsuit top. The stench of his body odor mixed with the usual stink of a moldy wetsuit prompted Jake to move upwind.

"Half-hour break?" Peter ventured.

"Whatever," Jake muttered, staring without interest at a stream that fed into the Cattibone across the river. Lying back on his life jacket, he studied colorless puffs of cloud against a cheerless blue sky until exhaustion forced him into a short doze.

"Jake, Jake, get up," Peter said. "Can moose swim?"

"Can who what?" sputtered Jake, rubbing his eyes.

"Can moose swim?"

Jake sat up to see a large, hairy moose sipping water from the stream at the other side of the river.

"I've heard they're meaner than grizzlies if they feel

like driving those racks into you. I've heard they'll crack all the bones of your body if they trample you," Peter continued. "Will that moose stay on his own side of the river?"

"Of course moose can swim, but why would one cross a rapid just to visit two smelly kayakers who are minding their own business? What time is it? Let's get this show back on the road."

Peter looked at his waterproof watch. "We've had only twenty-five minutes' rest. But I'm okay with that."

They nosed their kayaks back into the current and Jake splashed his face to wake up. Soon he and Peter found themselves tackling a long series of stomach-churning rapids. Here, Jake let Peter lead. The map wasn't joking when it labeled these Class $4\frac{1}{2}$. Jake felt at his limit. He was still pissed off with Peter but he felt safe following his skilled pick of routes. Sometimes, to nip his fears in the bud, Jake would pause in an eddy, examine the regiments of white waves crashing into one another ahead, and imagine the same rapid full of slalom gates, each one hung to ensure a boater's safety. Then, pretending he was at Nationals, he'd zigzag from one phantom gate to another, concentrating on one move at a time. Imagining a racecourse helped him conjure up an audience on shore and rescue boats at the finish. Anything, Jake thought, but the frightening sense of isolation, loss, and responsibility that was now his reality of the Cattibone's canyon.

Jake and Peter sped on for hours, until the sun sank beyond the high rim of the canyon walls and their hands were blistered from rotating their paddles. In the evening light, they approached a scary drop. Once again, the steep walls on both sides of the river ruled out scouting. Peter, taking the lead, dipped his paddle blades into the water as if testing a milkshake's thickness. He'd paddle a few strokes, spin upstream to slow himself down, and stroke against the current while looking back over his shoulder to memorize the location of obstacles that needed avoiding.

"Start middle right, do a U-turn around a tall gray boulder, then spin right and paddle for your life through a large hole," he shouted to Jake before disappearing over the horizon line. As Jake dropped through the upper part of the rapid, rounded the gray rock and started into a U-turn, he glimpsed Peter paused in a micro-eddy beyond a maze of small rocks toward the far left shore. Peter's arms were waving back and forth as if Jake was a jet plane he had to guide to an emergency landing.

"Why over there?" Jake muttered through clenched teeth. "Not a great place, buddy. How'd you get there, anyway? But I have to trust you, don't I?"

He completed the U-turn and pumped like crazy through the heart of the small hole. Then Jake stretched his right arm to its full length to sweep around a long, low rock. Instead of sneaking past the sentry, however, he felt himself slam sideways into it, and stick there like a nail on a magnet. His pulse shot up as he struggled to hold a slight downstream lean.

"Don't tip, don't tip," Jake said to his kayak through gritted teeth. The force of the water against the rock would hold him under water like a pressure hose and stop him from ejecting *or* rolling. And if that happened, he'd drown for sure.

Gingerly, he placed one hand on the rock, keeping the other around his paddle, and used all his strength to jiggle the boat forward. Just as the boat slid around the rock, the confused currents tipped him over and wrenched his paddle from his hands.

The cold water gave him an ice-cream headache as he held his breath and fought off the urge to panic. He was relieved to be free of the rock, but now he faced an unnerving challenge: rolling back up without his paddle. Hand-rolling was a difficult trick and he'd spent many hours practicing it in swimming pools. But, like most experienced kayakers, he could pull it off less than half the time, even in still water.

"Just do it!" he ordered himself, "before you wrap around another rock." Plastering his face against the deck of his boat, he placed one hand on top of the other, reached for the water surface, slapped with all the force he could muster, and arched his body around at the same time. Up came the boat, and up came his body. He gasped for air, saw that he was headed for a new hole, then felt Peter's paddle land neatly in his lap. Nice throw, Jake thought as he grabbed it and whipped his boat into a safe eddy only seconds before he would have been at the mercy of the hole without a paddle.

He worked himself the rest of the way to Peter and climbed out on a rock. From here, he spotted his own paddle spinning in a nearby eddy and waded out to retrieve it. What a stroke of luck. He didn't dare think what might have happened if the paddle had continued downstream. When he looked up again, he saw Peter hopping across channels of water, leading from rock to rock.

"What the…?" Then he saw it: the missing oar raft, curled like a candy wrapper around a giant offshore boulder.

Jake rushed to join Peter and together they swam to the rock that held the raft. They searched first for the sack that had held one of the trip's cellphones, but all they could find was some ripped strapping.

Their shoulders sank. Jake craved food, sleep, and something going right for once.

"If you ask me, we'll never get this raft off the rock by ourselves," Peter declared, voice flat. "Let's leave it. We've got more important business."

"*You* leave it," snapped Jake. "I'm pulling it off."

Jaw dropping, Peter placed his hands on his hips. "Jake, I know you're angry about what's happened, and I know I'm partly to blame, but it's time to get real and get on with things."

"What would you know about 'real'?" Jake demanded. "You're a spoiled little rich kid who's had everything handed to you on a golden platter for a little too long. Fancy kayaks, expensive cameras, exotic vacations. You don't earn anything, you don't appreciate anything, and all you think about is yourself. Everything for you is one big race or one big party. It's more important to show someone up — or get your photo in a magazine — than it is to be a friend or play by the safety rules. *Grow up*, Peter."

"*Me* grow up? It's time you grew up, Jake. You've had a chip on your shoulder ever since your dad took off —"

"*My dad's got nothing to do with this!*"

"— and you carry on like the world is plotting against you every moment of the day. Like you're some big martyr just because you have to work, like you have to win races because you hate the rest of the team, not because you enjoy the sport. You're so sour and negative and resentful that seagulls wouldn't poop on you! I had nothing to do with Angus's injury, or Ron getting out-of-his-mind drunk, or …"

Peter stopped, his face pale. Then he took a breath and continued. "As for this raft, it might as well be super-glued to that boulder. We'd need six strong men and machinery to peel it off, and how would you feel if Angus died while you tried to save a few strands of rubber?"

That triggered a new volcanic eruption. "A few strands of rubber?" Jake exploded, voice going hoarse. "Don't you understand, Peter? You killed Ron, made him destroy a raft worth thousands of dollars, probably pushed the company into bankruptcy — which affects numerous hard-working people's jobs, including mine — and spoiled every one of our passengers' holidays. That includes your parents' anniversary. *You* get real! *You* grow up! You learn to think about others' feelings and the way the other half lives." He took a deep breath. "If we leave this raft, the next change in water level will take it downstream again, and rocks will puncture the other chambers until it disappears. Sam doesn't have dozens of rafts. He can't afford to lose one. We could pull it off and secure it somewhere above the waterline in just a few minutes if you'd shut up and help for once!"

Jake leaned down, picked up a rock and threw it with full force at Peter. Peter ducked as the missile whistled over his head, stared at Jake and stormed out of reach. He launched his boat and disappeared.

12   Mishap at Dusk

Peter parked himself in an eddy downstream and craned his neck around a rock so he could watch Jake without Jake seeing him. Peter was shaking all over, and his head throbbed so violently he felt dizzy. He knew all too well that everyone at Sam's Adventure Tours hated him, Jake most of all. He knew they had some cause. He shouldn't have stolen Ron's kayak, although given another half hour, he'd have had it back at camp and no one would have been the wiser. Except Neeta. So gullible. The perfect accomplice. But he'd never have put her in danger. Jake had no right to say he'd "used" her in the same breath as accusing him of murder. She hadn't even been injured when the dead tree got pulled in, and that was a *freak* thing, just like the log that got Ron. Jake wouldn't even admit that Ron had been drinking, wouldn't admit it was Ron's bad judgment to row so close to the falls, combined with the *totally freak* chance of a log hitting him at exactly the wrong second.

The guy didn't have a chance, especially without a helmet, but none of that was Peter's fault, couldn't they see?

Peter pressed his forehead to his kayak's cold deck and rocked back and forth. Okay, so it was partly his fault. He shouldn't have stolen the kayak, shouldn't have dragged Neeta into things. Should have helped Jake more during the trip to ease tensions between them. Shouldn't have said all that nasty stuff a few minutes ago.

Peter lifted his head and wriggled his toes, which were numb from sitting without movement for too many hours. He'd thought he could redeem himself by doing this emergency run fast and clean — getting Jake and himself safely to a source of help. He'd thought that would make everything right. Now he realized the real reasons Jake hated him. Yes, he'd been a jerk. Yes, his love of racing and risk-taking had made him blind to safety rules, and, well, rules of friendship. But he'd had some time to think while bobbing along in that raft the last few days. And he'd realized something about Jake's situation that had never struck him before. Jake's dad. He hadn't just left a few years ago. *He'd left with no explanation.* He'd rejected Jake the same time as the Montpetit family had taken off. A two-for-one cut. Maybe some things you just don't get over, especially when they're fused in your mind.

So Jake had to reject someone or something back. Was that it? And Peter had set himself up as the perfect target, not that he'd meant to. He'd thought Jake was jealous of his race success. Stupid. Part of his jerk-self to think that, he could see now. But Peter wasn't going to let Jake push him away the way Jake's father had pushed away his family. Not just because the two had to work together to get down this canyon, not just to save Angus, but because... well, something to do with rules of friendship. Something to do with a different kind of risk. Something to do with going the distance.

Peter snapped off his sprayskirt and crawled out of his kayak. He worked his way back up to where Jake was swimming and rock-hopping between two boulders, arranging ropes into a complicated "Z" configuration that included a section tied to metal rings on the sides of the damaged raft. Aha, the ol' Z system for pulling wrapped boats off rocks. Like most kayakers, Peter had heard of it but never learned it.

Jake was pulling on the ropes like a crazed man. And getting no response. Peter watched him pit all his strength against the rope. Again, nothing budged. He strained and grunted and pulled from different angles, mindless of the sweat pouring down his face as if certain the raft would soon give way.

Peter coughed. Jake swung around. "Maybe I can help. Gosh, we sure could use that moose now, eh?"

Jake made room for him and the two threw their weight into the tug-o-war with the raft. Slowly, reluctantly, a corner of it lifted.

"Again!" Jake shouted. Again they heaved, straining until they felt more rubber give way and Jake could fiddle with his system.

"One more time!" they chanted, and sure enough, the collapsed raft gave up its rocky embrace and skied across the water toward the boys, perched on an upstream boulder.

"I'm sorry," Jake said, after a few minutes. "I didn't mean all of that."

"Yes you did and I s'pose I deserved it. But I didn't mean everything I said about you," Peter said, eyes averted. "Sometimes I'm kinda jealous of you. You're way better at — well, at reading people's feelings, and you always know what you want and how to get it. Anyway, so I've thought about what you said, and I'll keep thinking about it." He glanced up, then quickly away again. "I'm saying I know I've got stuff to work on. Is that a deal?" He extended his arm.

"Deal," Jake said, extending his own hand with a smile. "And I'll try for an attitude change, if you'll bear with me."

Peter grinned. "Speaking of bears, where are we going to camp tonight without worrying about them? We've got no tent and I'm no good at rubbing sticks together. It'll be dark in an hour and we're both pooped."

"We'll worry about that when we're too tired to paddle another stroke. I'll start the fire for no extra charge if you'll help me haul this baby above the high-water mark. Oh," Jake added, "thanks for throwing me your paddle and saving me from a bad swim."

"It's okay. Let's just hope you don't need to repay the favor before we get off this river. It's pretty intense, huh?"

"Yeah." In the fading light, they broke out some food and stuffed their faces while discussing whether to paddle another rapid before making camp.

Peter examined Nancy's map. "I'd say we're here, which would mean we've paddled roughly half the canyon in one day — that's forty-seven miles. Totally impressive." He reached out to slap Jake on the back.

Jake grinned and patted Peter on the head. "We're an awesome team. What can I say?"

"So would you agree we shoot for finishing off the canyon tomorrow night?" Peter continued. "And I'd sleep better if we put this next big one behind us now. The map calls it One-Mile Rapid. Class 4."

"Let's do it," Jake agreed. The two boys stuffed gear back into their kayak flotation bags, designed to double as waterproof stuff sacks.

As its name implied, One-Mile Rapid was a long and hairy one. Jake led, and Peter, buoyed by his renewed friendship with Jake, followed. He was glad about the gentle warm-up the accelerating water first offered. But all too soon, the canyon walls threw dark shadows across a seething blanket of white that wriggled toward them. As Jake's boat entered the battle zone and Peter struggled to keep him in sight, the currents churned with greater fury. The faster Peter dodged rocks, waves, and holes, the faster they came at him. Like a kid gripping a joystick at a video arcade, Peter tried steering his ship between flying objects by hanging left and right turns at dizzying speed. But each time he averted a collision, the game seemed to shift him to a higher level. His mouth was as dry as his body was wet, and though he'd never have admitted it to Jake, his nerves felt ready to collapse.

Halfway through the rapid, a massive wave shoved him — into a hole that turned out the lights. Upside-down. *Great.* Determined not to let the river win, Peter rolled and grabbed a breath. The hole still held him — and knocked him over again. Again he rolled, and again it punched him down. This time, he felt himself twisted like laundry in a washing machine, unable to get a proper grip on the paddle or find a position that would give him the leverage he needed. His lungs screamed for oxygen.

He took one hand off his paddle and reached for

the loop on the end of his sprayskirt with the other. If the hole wouldn't relinquish his boat with him inside it, he had no choice but to eject and try to swim out. One yank and he was free, somersaulting downwards out of his cockpit, deeper into the hole. It battered him full force as he kept one stranglehold on his paddle, another on his tumbling boat. As his head surfaced above the foam, he snatched a badly needed breath and waited for water to fill his boat. The added ballast, he hoped, would buy him a ticket out of this cauldron, while the kayak's flotation bags would ensure that the boat didn't sink. That was the plan — every kayaker's backup when trapped in a hole. Just as Peter was losing heart, the boat pointed skywards and shot out with just enough power to drag along its hitchhiker. Pain shot through his arm as the heavy boat tugged him, and the bone-chilling cold of the river threatened to stop his heart. But Peter lost no time working his way to the upstream end of the boat and lifting his feet up to the surface.

"Feet up and downstream." Jake's safety-talk voice echoed to him.

Within seconds, he realized he was nowhere near the end of the rapid, nowhere near a safe eddy, and that a long, cold, and bruising swim awaited him if Jake couldn't help. Then he spotted his buddy hovering nearby, paddle poised in an uneasy patch of calm. Jake gave Peter a reassuring nod and paddled his way.

Although Peter could see that upcoming currents were going to make a rescue difficult, he grabbed the end of Jake's boat. For a quarter mile, the duo bobbed through the rapids, Jake negotiating monstrous waves and tight moves, Peter fighting to maintain his grip on the two boats and his paddle even as the cold sapped his strength.

"Let go!" he heard Jake scream as the two headed for a hole that threatened to swamp the rescuer. The instant he obeyed, Peter felt himself sucked into the angry hole — and he saw Jake capsize.

"Please roll, Jake. Please roll," Peter prayed. The river gods saw fit to toss and kick and bruise Peter like a football deep underwater. But Peter was more worried about Jake than himself. "Two of us swimming at once — the worse possible scenario. Don't let it happen, Jake. Roll." And then the millions of bubbles that were pressed against Peter's face, hands, and body dashed off like a frightened school of fish. The hole delivered one final, swift kick that chucked him out to where gentler currents grabbed and floated him to a mid-river eddy.

Peter hauled himself up onto a flat rock and looked upstream and downstream. Jake was nowhere in sight. Was he still in the hole? In or out of his boat?

Had he made it to the end of One-Mile Rapid? Peter's teeth chattered and every pore ached. He struggled to shift his limbs to a more comfortable position and to yank his boat and paddle up to join him.

"If I don't get something warm on and some calories down my throat, I'm going to lose it," he thought. He fumbled for his waterproof bag and shook his jacket and an energy bar onto the flat boulder. As his taste buds wrapped themselves around the food, Peter looked up the river again.

"Jake, where are you? It'll be dark in minutes. What are we going to do?" A lump rose to his throat, and it had nothing to do with the energy bar. The river blurred to an unfocused picture, and it wasn't just the dusk. To paddle the Cattibone alone … he felt a crushing pressure on his chest. How asinine that fight had been, how childish his behavior all trip. How dependent he and Jake had become on each other the past twelve hours. Alone? No, please no.

Peering further upstream, Peter spied a strange rock formation — a short, crude Stonehenge-like arch barely above water — with a small figure atop it. As Peter leaned forward and cocked his head, the figure moved. Could it be? Yes, it was — Jake, upright but helpless inside his boat, which formed a tenuous bridge just above water between two river rocks.

Peter dropped his energy bar. "Oh my god. He's bridged. He's okay, but he's bridged."

The two rocks holding bow and stern prisoner were both out of Jake's reach. Clearly, he'd rolled up with unlucky timing and gotten caught sideways to the current. Peter eyed the strong current between Jake and himself and the sheer walls on either side of the river. He had no hope of getting to his friend, and without Peter's help, Jake had two grim choices. One was to let himself tip over, then eject, dropping headfirst into the river and leaving the boat behind while swimming for safety. This would leave the boys with half the canyon still to paddle and only one boat between them. The other was to peel off his sprayskirt and crawl along the length of his boat to one of the rocks holding it. Chances were the boat would roll over like a log, dumping him into the drink while remaining stuck solid. But if he could gain a foothold on one of the rocks, maybe he could lift the boat off and relaunch.

Peter, taking his rescue rope out of his boat, shouted to Jake above the din of the rapid and saw his friend turn toward him. They were too far apart to communicate with words, and in moments it would be too dark to communicate with gestures, but Peter was certain Jake understood his options. He watched as Jake snapped off his sprayskirt, lifted his bum, and squatted delicately on his kayak stern, every muscle concentrated on maintaining his balance. Now, moving like Indiana Jones on a ledge over a snakepit, Jake began to crawl over his bow toward the rock. For one panicky second, the boat wobbled, and Jake's paddle, which he had been inching along ahead of him, clattered off the deck and into the river. Jake froze, but Peter grabbed his own paddle and, dropping onto his stomach, reached it out into the currents to snag Jake's paddle as it floated by. He breathed easy again only when he had pulled both their paddles safely onto his rock.

Turning back upstream, Peter watched Jake's dark silhouette resume the slow-motion crawl, reaching out for the rock ahead. At long last, he grabbed it and pulled the rest of his long body over the wavering kayak until he was standing safely on the rock.

In the final light, Jake's shadowy figure turned and gave a thumb's-up to Peter, then leaned over and put all his muscle into tugging the stern of the stuck boat off the opposite boulder. It took several tries, and when the boat suddenly popped off, Jake lost his balance and plunged into the dark river with it. Peter, who had been half-expecting this, waited until Jake had hold of his runaway boat and was a little way upstream before tossing the rescue rope. Once Jake gripped the rope, Peter reeled him in like the prize catch of his life, before downstream currents could tear him away. Then, kneeling to reduce his own chances of being pulled back into the river, Peter pulled Jake and his waterlogged kayak atop his rock, which now held two boats, two boys and two paddles. They hugged long and hard without a trace of embarrassment. But as they sat down and shook a new energy bar out of Peter's bag, the last of the day's light vanished.

"It's too dark to run the rest of this rapid safely," Peter pointed out.

"And this rock is too small to spend the night on," Jake observed.

"Lucky for us the night is clear. When the moon comes up, it'll be nearly full. I say we hang out here till that happens, then finish One-Mile Rapid and camp anywhere we can. Until then, it's time for a picnic on this poor excuse for an island. Yes?"

"A lunatic picnic," came the response.

13 The Cave

Just before he fell asleep that night, Jake mentally assigned the birds to wake him up at dawn. He and Peter had pulled off the river at the end of One-Mile Rapid on a cramped beach. Clouds had obscured the moon as soon as they landed, and the night smelled of rain. With no tent, Jake just hoped the rain would hold off until morning.

"At least we're safe from bears here," he assured Peter, swatting mosquitoes as he tugged his sleeping bag from his boat. "There's no way one could get down these cliffs."

Chucking handfuls of dried apricots into their mouths and gulping some water, the two collapsed into a deep sleep, too tired to light a fire.

Unfortunately, birds don't do wake-up calls when a rainstorm rolls in. So Peter and Jake were awakened instead by the splatter of raindrops on their sleeping bags.

"Yikes," said Jake, springing up. "My bag isn't waterproof and I need it dry tonight."

He shook off the water and stuffed his bag into its waterproof sack, shivering as he pulled out his fleece jacket. "Get up, lazy," he needled Peter. "It's getting light."

"*My* bag is waterproof and that gives me another hour's sleep," Peter mumbled. "Besides, you promised me a fire. I'll have that with eggs and hash browns, please."

Jake searched his kayak for his water bottle to pour over his friend's face. Instead, he pulled out two squashed tangerines and two energy bars, and dropped one each on Peter.

"They're mine if you're not up in five minutes."

Peter tore the wrapper off his bar with his teeth and chewed off a chunk. "These things don't even start to do the job, do they? We're wasting away, Jake." He rolled down his sleeping bag and pressed a thumb and index finger into his stomach. "Can't even pinch it," he whined, though a smile tugged at the corner of his mouth. "I'm positively skeletal, Jake old buddy. How about a steak, eggs, and pancake breakfast the first morning outta here?"

"Stop!" Jake protested. "No mention of food allowed!" He closed his eyes and stuck his tongue out to catch some raindrops. "But we can always *think* about it."

A short while later, the duo climbed into their kayaks and set out in the gray drizzle, which soon increased to a downpour. Today, Jake was glad of Peter's company, happy to chatter back and forth between rapids, happy for Peter's strength and optimism. But after hours of being pelted by rain, he found it hard to keep his mind off what lay ahead.

"This is going to raise the river level if it keeps up all day," Peter called out.

"Yeah, but if we paddle till dark, we should be near the end of the canyon."

"We have a biggie today, right?"

"Yup, a Class 5 called Blender at the very end of the canyon. Nancy said there's a killer hole three-quarters of the way across the rapid that we don't want to go near, and a small, twisty route on the right we have to make. There's no way to carry around it. Cliffs lean out both sides of the river a long way before, she said. We can scout only from a distance. Half the trick will be getting there before dark. I'm sure not going to tackle that one with the lights out."

"You've got *that* right," Peter agreed, churning the water faster.

The rain refused to let up all day, and the boys' only breaks were for drinks of water. They kept filling the bottles from the Cattibone and popping water purification tablets in, though this inspired Peter to make faces and stick his tongue out. "Yech."

Although hunger gnawed at Jake's ribs, he swore he could survive this ordeal for Angus's sake.

Despite being tired and hungry, the two made good time. By mid-afternoon, they reckoned they were only a few miles from Blender when Jake insisted on a rest. Nancy's map had marked a cave here, and while there clearly wasn't time to explore it, he was dying for a peek inside. It might take his mind off his aching wrists and back and his numb feet. Too many hours in the rain, Jake thought. We deserve a moment's shelter.

Jake spotted the cave's entrance from the river and whooped when he noted raspberry bushes either side of it. "Peter, there's a double feature playing here. How fast can we eat a bushel of berries and poke our noses into a cave Nancy seemed to think worth marking on her map?"

"Alright! A cave to explore! And if we haven't earned half an hour's break, we never will," Peter replied. "Leave no raspberries on the bush, I say!"

The two sprinted up the beach to thrust their arms and faces into the thorny bushes.

Soon Jake patted his swelled gut and said, "That's all I can take. For ten minutes, that is. I'll top up when we come back out of the cave. Grab the flashlights from the boats, Peter. I can hardly wait to get out of this downpour!"

Jake ducked to enter the arched tunnel, and with

his head low to keep from bumping it, he padded along its dry, silty floor. Peter followed right behind, kicking small piles of rocks out of his way. Jake ran a hand along the cold, sculpted walls and shone his flashlight into shadowed crevices. After a few minutes, the ceiling rose enough to allow the boys to straighten up.

A faint rumble sounded from down the corridor, like a drum roll announcing the visitors. Its volume rose steadily as they progressed.

"I'm guessing a waterfall," Jake said. The corridor made his voice sound as if it were coming out of a tin can.

Curious, they kept going until a fine mist doused their faces. Jake's ears fastened on the drum roll's crescendo. Definitely a waterfall, he decided, face glowing. He imagined a massive gallery filled with glittering rock formations. He'd visited commercial caves with colorful spotlights trained on icicle-like stalactites and stalagmites, and clear, turquoise ponds that disappeared into secret tunnels of whitewater. There, guides had shone powerful flashlights on stunning crystals and led tours along roped-off walkways and sturdy suspension bridges.

A draft tickled his face. He shivered in the freezing temperature and wiped droplets of water from his face. Peter's hand touched his shoulder.

"Not much further. We have to watch our time."

Jake's boots crunched to a stop, but the waterfall beckoned. "Just a few steps more," he insisted. "Then we'll rest and still be back at the boats on the half-hour mark."

"Okay," Peter agreed. They rounded a corner and lifted their faces to a strong new breeze, half humid, half cold. They pushed forward, flashlight beams trained ahead, the waterfall's pounding matching their heartbeats, and suddenly found themselves on a ledge six feet over the floor of a vast gallery. A single shaft of muted daylight fell from a small opening in the eight-storey-high domed ceiling above. A layered waterfall spilled from a dark lip far across the cathedral-sized room, feeding a stream that meandered across the cratered, rock-strewn floor and disappeared into a tunnel. Otherworldly formations filled the cave like a sculptor's work-in-progress: long, needle-like cones hanging from the ceiling, fat teeth rising from the floor to meet them, delicate straws decorating every nook and cranny, and fat, flowing figures that resembled melted-wax monsters.

Upwards swooped Jake's flashlight, capturing swallows in their mud-and-straw nests, then over to a side chamber beneath the vaulted ceiling, where a small cluster of bats quivered. And then, playing the light along crevices in the walls and ceiling, the boys illuminated what appeared to be an upside-down garden of cauliflower heads: gypsum flowers of calcite.

"Awesome," Peter shouted above the water noise.

"Awesome, awesome, awesome," echoed the shrouded figures.

The boys flopped themselves down on their tummies, elbows propped on the view ledge, and played their flashlights around the subterranean wonderland. They paused only to drink from their water bottles and break their last sandwich in half. They'd hardly finished this off when Peter nudged his buddy in the ribs.

"It's time," he said. "Remember Blender, Angus, the Cattibone? We gotta get outta here if we want to do Blender before dark."

"It's dark now," said Jake, switching off his flashlight with a teasing smile. But a shudder traveled down his body as he realized how little relief from total blackness the tiny skylight offered. He flicked the flashlight back on but didn't budge. He was putting the finishing touches on a plan that had occurred to him the moment they'd laid down on the ledge. Jake trained his beam on a far wall beneath the dome, then ran it up and down the wall supporting their ledge.

"Follow me," he ordered Peter, jumping up, turning around, plastering his hands against the edge of the ledge, and lowering himself down until he could jump to the gallery floor.

"Whaa?" Peter protested. "No way! Have you lost your mind? We're supposed to be going!"

"I'm starving. We both are. Give me another thirty minutes and I'll have your eggs and hash browns ready — in a manner of speaking. And then we'll be out of here, back to our boats, doing Blender in daylight. I promise."

"Jake, you've gone berserk. I'm worried about you."

"*Are you hungry?*" Jake repeated, breaking into a trot across the chamber's moonscape. He soon registered the sound of Peter's footsteps behind him as he dodged from one human-sized stalagmite, column, or boulder to another, flashlight illuminating their eerie stances. At the base of the waterfall, Jake paused to dip his hands into the cold flow. Sweet pureness flowed over his tongue and down his throat. Soon, he and Peter were plunging their heads into the flow to gulp faces full. They laughed as the water sloshed past the berries in their mostly empty stomachs to gurgle in rude harmony.

"How can a little ribbon of water make this much noise?" Jake shouted.

"Where's the food?" Peter shouted back.

Jake gazed up at the amphitheater's ceiling, where swallows flashed past the shaft of softening daylight and pointed to rock shelves just off the waterfall, two-thirds the way up the gallery.

"Eggs over easy?" he suggested, placing a neoprene boot in a smooth indentation in the waterfall and hauling himself upwards. Peter sank back with his mouth hanging open as Jake climbed, agile as a cat, higher and higher, never quite touching the water plunging down alongside him, never hesitating in his steady progress toward the nests. Peter held his breath as his friend reached the ledge, plopped himself down on it as casually as an old lady on a park bench, and motioned Peter to follow.

"I'm not a climber," Peter shouted with cupped hands. He covered his ears as the echo mocked his words. "I'm afraid of heights."

Jake swung his feet like a kid. "I'm not a climber either, but it's a breeze — really. It's not slippery like outdoor waterfalls, and the water has washed away loose rocks. Come on!"

"Come on! Come on! Come on!" the canyon mimicked. Peter stuck a trembling foot into a crevice and fumbled for a handhold.

Meanwhile, Jake slid sideways on his slab, feet still fanning the clammy air five storeys above the cave's floor. He ignored the annoying little birds that rose and screeched at him. First in line at the help-yourself buffet, he pocketed every egg he could reach, nesting them in his paddling jacket pocket with all the gentleness of a mother swallow. Just as an unsteady Peter appeared, stiff and frozen on the far end of the ledge, Jake wriggled back and motioned Peter to climb into a crack in the wall behind them.

Peter, clutching the wall with a white face, half-closed his eyes as he tumbled backwards into the cavity. "Didn't want to free-fall onto the world's largest bed of nails," he muttered.

"Huh?"

Peter jerked his head toward the forest of stalagmites far below, eyes squeezed shut. Jake, mindful of his fragile cache, lifted one leg at a time into the tiny grotto, and pointed to a large square rock.

"Perfect picnic table," he declared as he produced his treasure: eight unbroken eggs.

"Crack!" went the first, as Jake slurped down every drop. Crack, crack, crack came seven more breaks in the alcove's quiet, as a small portion of the cave's next swallow generation donated energy to two ravenous boys.

Buoyed by this unexpected meal, Peter hung his head out of the cramped space and peered upwards at the hole in the domed ceiling still three storeys above them.

"What a place," he said, shaking his head in wonder. He crawled back to the stone slab and shone his flashlight on the walls of their balcony room.

"We're in Hansel and Gretel's cave," Peter said, moving to the rear wall.

"Eh?"

"The walls are made of marshmallows. Here, have one." He tore off a piece of soft, puffy white, formed it into a ball, and tossed it at Jake. Jake caught it and put his tongue against it. The bitter, salty taste made him cringe, which prompted Peter to laugh.

Jake pinched the softness between his fingers. "It is like a marshmallow."

"Moon milk. I remember a caver at a school assembly telling us about it. Imagine me remembering something from a school assembly!" he added. "It's calcite. Better not disturb any more. They take like thousands of years to grow."

He checked his watch. "And it's gonna take us thousands of years to get off the Cattibone if we don't climb down and outta here, now. One hour since we entered this cave, Jake Evans. Lead out. *No more arguing!*"

Jake nodded, slung his leg over the balcony and swung his flashlight one last time around the gallery. A galaxy of stars met his gaze. Every drop of water on the end of every stalactite winked. It wasn't a spooky cave, he decided. Though he wouldn't have wanted to spend the night up here above the ghost figures. He shimmied down the falls, then coached a petrified Peter.

14   The Logs' Promise

As they burst out of the entry tunnel, both boys grabbed another handful of raspberries before striding to their kayaks. Though instantly drenched by the rainfall they'd almost forgotten about, they hardly noticed.

"Mmm, raw eggs and raspberries," Peter grinned, patting his belly. "Who'd've thought? Thanks, Jake. I still hate heights but it was worth it for the protein."

Peter secured his sprayskirt, picked up his paddle, and glanced at his wristwatch. "We're gonna have to motor it to get through Blender by dark. Then we can *really* relax. Tomorrow morning it's just flat water all the way to the bus, right?"

Jake smiled and nodded. The awkwardness between them was gone.

Peter welcomed the familiar feel of shoehorning himself into his kayak and peeling out into the waves. Never mind that his shoulders ached, his fingers were blistered, and he was low on sleep. Never mind that the most dangerous rapid of the trip lay just ahead. With a little more fuel in his system thanks to Jake and the knowledge they could be out of the canyon tonight, nothing could dampen his enthusiasm. The raindrops could just as well have been sunrays.

And yet, as dusk fell, his anxiousness returned. Soon, an ominous rumble downstream notified Peter where they were.

"Blender marks the end of the canyon," Jake reminded him. "If we survive her, we're home-free. Who's first?"

Peter could tell Jake was hoping he would lead the way. "We need to check her out."

"We won't be able to see much this far away, but I'm willing to scramble over rocks if you are," said Jake. They found an eddy that let them climb out and lift their boats onto a shelf in the canyon wall. They crept along the edge of nervous eddies, jumping from rock to rock, feeling for handholds while trying not to hit their heads on the arched wall or slip into the furious river. When they rounded a bend and met a sharp point that ran out into heavy current, they had to halt. The bend at least gave them a faraway glimpse of Blender's bottom hole, a cauldron of raging water the width of three head-to-toe kayaks. Peter's heart bounced up to his throat, and he gripped the cliff as if it were moving. The dizzy feeling he'd had in the cave had returned. The boys shifted their gaze to the far right, only to witness a ghastly sight. A giant cedar had floated down the river and lodged itself firmly across the only passable route — and not a single eddy afforded safe harbor near it.

Peter looked at Jake. Jake looked at Peter. Had they come this far only to be blocked and stranded? Their options now appeared bleak, indeed. They would have to risk the hole, or work their way back upstream until they could climb a cliff or wait for rescue. And when would that be? In a few days if Jim and his party made it through. Peter watched as Jake leaned his forehead on his fist and studied the hole again. He wondered what was going on in that shrewd mind of his, wondered if he felt as deflated as he did.

"What would I give for a pair of binoculars right now?" said Jake. He strained his neck as far as he could and shaded his eyes with one hand. "The rain has brought the river up. Sometimes that washes out a hole that's deadly at lower levels. I think we're running this river way higher than Nancy described."

"Uh huh," agreed Peter. "And your point is …?"

"My point is maybe there's a way through the hole we can't see. My point is that we're unlikely to make it up a cliff even if we had days and climbing equipment for it."

"Or we could outfit the front of our boats with chainsaws and cut our way through the tree." Peter saw Jake bristle but obviously decide to let the sarcasm go.

"Peter, you know how kayakers on exploratory trips push logs into the current to see if and how fast a hole lets the tree trunks through?"

"Yeah," said Peter and rolled his eyes. All he could think about was leaping into the kayak and powering through that impossible hole. Even a huge risk would be worth ending the uncertainty they were in right now. "Oh great, Jake. You think we've got nothing better to do than play Pooh-sticks? That's what they call it in England, you know, named after Winnie the Pooh."

"Peter, please be serious," Jake begged. "This is an emergency run to save Angus's life. And this is a rapid that could kill us if we don't think it through."

"As if I don't know that. Haven't you figured out by now I try to lighten things up when I'm totally terrified? Humor is my sick way of handling the fear factor. Okay, I'll collect a pile of small logs. Where's a beaver dam when you need one?" Taking care to locate firm grips for their hands and feet in the fading light, the two made their way back to their kayaks. From there, they plodded upstream and downstream, numb feet splashing, sometimes tripping as they waded along the edge of the river through unrelenting rain until they had hauled five small logs into the viewpoint eddy. Peter pushed the first one out into the current with a long stick.

"And it's Knobby, folks, out of the starting gate and hugging the inside of the track, head up and proud. Oops! She's bumped into a rock, but she's still in there, folks, a determined little filly. She's picking up speed now, ready to leap that hurdle. Go right, Knobby, more to the right! Thataway. She jumps, and … oh no, it's not a pretty sight. Ouch! She's on her hind legs and looking battered. But will our Knobby cross the finish line? Yes! There she is, folks, none-the-worse for wear, breathing hard, a little bruised, and cruising right on out of sight. A record twenty-five seconds. Was that good or what?"

"You're weird, Peter," Jake said. Peter watched him trying to hide a grin while pushing in the second log. One by one, the boys watched their missiles strike the hole. Two were down for a count of forty seconds, tossed about like matchsticks as they spun in the undertow. All five logs eventually reappeared, however, one in a matter of only fifteen seconds. The kayakers tried to memorize the line of the fifteen-second log.

"So, assuming our kayaks are roughly the same weight as these logs and we can hold our breath for forty seconds while being put through the rinse cycle, theoretically, we have a five-out-of-five chance of surviving, right? That's the logs' promise? When Blender finishes liquidating us, we simply float out, roll up, and carry on?"

"That's the plan," Jake confirmed in a low, solemn voice. The two studied each other for long moments, then began timing themselves on holding their breath. Neither could make it past forty seconds. Finally, they shook hands. Peter noticed that both their hands were clammy.

"To hell with U.S. or Canadian Nationals," he said. "Ahead of us is the competition of a lifetime. Tell you what. If you forgive me for everything up to today, I'll go first."

"Deal."

Peter took one long, last look at Blender and picked his way back to his boat. He headed out, paddling slowly, boat diagonal to where the greatest flow of current tumbled by. With a smart salute, he spun his boat around and began to sprint, determined to hit the center-right of the hole at warp speed. What Jake couldn't see from his eddy was Peter crash into the foam like a race-car driver against the barriers. Up shot the kayak into the air, only to perform a harrowing back flip. Shoved helmet-first into the center of the spinning cocoon, yanked with terrific violence this way and that, Peter would later tell Jake he'd never felt a force so determined to pry him from his boat, sprayskirt and all. Hanging upside-down, gripping his paddle shaft with all his might, holding his pressure-washed face as tightly as he could against the deck of his boat, Peter waited, counted, and prayed.

He counted to forty as his lungs threatened to burst. When he knew his time was up, knew the hole was not going to relinquish him as planned, he made a desperate attempt to Eskimo roll within Blender's stomach. He came up just far enough to grasp a breath before the water tore his paddle away from him.

And that, as it turned out, was his undoing.

15   The Clearing

Jake sat in the upper eddy for what seemed a lifetime but in reality was only thirty seconds. He knew the time because Peter had loaned him his watch, and the two had agreed that Jake would leave the eddy exactly thirty seconds after Peter was out of sight. That way, if Peter washed out of the hole without his boat, Jake would be close enough behind to rescue him, assuming Jake punched through in shape to do a rescue. And if Peter blasted through and rolled okay, he'd find an eddy fast, scramble up the bank, and anchor a rescue rope in case Jake needed help. Of course, if Peter and his boat were still in the hole when Jake hit it, there'd be nothing Jake could do but crash into him and hope the nasty hole would spit them both out eventually.

Jake tried to shake off such thoughts as he clenched his paddle. He took long, deep breaths to still his trembling body. Finally, he shot across the eddy line like an arrow leaving a bow. As he accelerated toward Blender, he wrapped his mind around what the logs had looked like as he and Peter had fed them through. We'll be okay, he told himself. The logs promised.

"Trust yourself for reading the currents," Angus had told him. That memory bolstered Jake's courage. With a single scan, he surveyed every patch of foam in the crazy quilt of turbulence around him and dug in with all he had.

"Here I come, Blender," Jake shouted. "Let me through!"

Unknowingly selecting a line just left of where Peter had dropped into the hole, Jake sprinted like a madman and threw himself into the massive wave, felt himself enveloped by the tempest, felt his bow plunge deeply into its heart. Even as the far wall of water slowed his kayak to a near standstill, Jake lifted one arm high and speared the wave again, this time with a forward reach of his paddle blade, grabbing for a hold inside the angry curler. "Gotcha," he thought. "I'm yours, and you're mine. Now what're you going to do?" For a microsecond, his boat stalled against the wet, swollen lip. Then it tilted upwards, straining for an exit, fighting against a backward slide into the center. Jake closed his eyes and leaned further forward, hanging on like a rodeo performer on a bucking bronco. As his arm muscles stretched to a snapping point, he kept his blade deep in the monster's belly until slowly, that blade lifted him, boat and all, over the frothy white and into a world with gray sky, green shoreline, and calm eddies. He was out of the canyon! With heaving chest, he shook the water from his eyes and scanned the river.

First, he spotted Peter crawling from the river's edge up onto a muddy bank. Next, through the curtain of rain, he noted Peter's boat pressed against tree roots hanging out over the river. Finally, he sighted Peter's paddle — which was odd because Peter never let go of his paddle — bobbing merrily downstream.

"I'll be right back," Jake called out. He sprinted to the paddle, scooped it up, and threw it like a javelin to shore. Next, he struggled back upstream and pushed the nose of his boat into Peter's boat, which had just broken free of the roots.

"Back into the eddy we go," he coaxed it. Within minutes, he'd hauled both boats up on shore and placed the paddles beside them. He worried, as he hiked back to Peter, that his friend had not moved from the spot where he'd first seen him. Peter sat, feet still in the water, eyes downcast, holding one arm across his chest.

"Are you hurt?"

"It's my shoulder." Peter bit his lip and turned his face away. "I think it got pulled right out of its socket."

Jake sat beside him in the mud and rain. "Can you move your shoulder at all?"

"No."

"So you've dislocated it. Peter, I know how to put dislocated shoulders back in. We learned in first-aid training. It'll hurt like hell for a few minutes, but the sooner we do it, the better, before it swells. Then we'll put it in a sling. You'll be able to move it again in twenty-four hours."

"If it has to be done and you know how, then get it over with," Peter said through gritted teeth.

Jake helped his buddy to his feet, stood behind him, and reached his arm over Peter's to grasp the wrist of the injured limb. "Take a deep breath," he instructed. As soon as Peter sucked in the breath, Jake swiveled the arm out by its elbow, lifted it high until he heard a sickening "pop," lowered it, and returned it to a sling position.

With the very first movement, Peter let out a shrill cry and continued screaming in broken gasps for several minutes. Jake felt cruel as Peter's face turned white and gray, but soon, Peter fell silent and dropped to his knees, clutching his arm protectively as if expecting Jake to launch a second assault.

"It went back in nicely," Jake said. "It'll feel tons better by tomorrow night. We'll camp here for now. When you're ready, let's get into the trees and see if we can rig up a way to sleep dry tonight. I'll grab the boats."

Peter nodded and, after a while, stood and followed

Jake, who whistled a tune to help raise Peter's spirits while dragging the two heavy kayaks, a paddle sticking out of each.

When Jake noticed Peter wincing each time they hit uneven ground, he whipped off his paddling jacket to make a sling.

"Stay here a minute while I look around," he said, then moved deeper into the woods, looking for a thick stand of trees. A few minutes later, he was startled to bump into an overgrown clearing with a gathering of derelict plank houses. Except for mossy roofs half fallen-in and heavy doors hanging askew, the clutch of shacks resembled a re-created historical native village. Tumbledown fish-drying racks leaned against the one-room houses, and circular pits marked semi-underground storage caches, now half filled with mud and pine cones.

Jake pushed open the door of the nearest cabin and saw two pairs of built-in bunk beds along the walls and a small iron stove near the single, broken window. A rusty washbasin perched on a stool in one corner. Rain poured through a hole in the ceiling near the door and ran out through a hole in the floor directly below. The place smelled terribly musty, but the roof immediately above the bunks remained intact.

"Peter!" Jake shouted, dropping their belongings on the floor and sprinting back to lead his friend through the near-darkness. Peter looked over the clearing with a dazed expression and stepped into the cabin. He gripped his arm, squared his jaw, and lay down on a lower bunk. Jake helped him out of his wetsuit and into thermals and his sleeping bag, fished some aspirin out of the first-aid kit, and refashioned an arm sling out of some gauze.

Flashlight in hand, he stepped out into the rain to look around more. To his delight, he ran into a bush loaded with ripe berries.

"Ripe blueberries!" He scooped them off branches by the handful and sank his face into his filled palms. When he'd had his fill, he lay his paddling jacket like a tarp under the bush and shook and stroked the branches till he'd collected several cups of the juicy berries. He marched back into the cabin and helped Peter sit up to eat.

"You're the best," Peter said, but his voice was a tired monotone and he only picked at the berries. Soon he lay down and tucked his sleeping bag up to his chin.

"Jake," he said after a while, "what would the rafts have done if they'd made it to Blender?"

"Scouted the rapid like we did, rowed the oar raft through the hole first, and set up a throw-rope rescue system for the rest," Jake replied. "Rafts are bigger and heavier. They can make it through things kayaks can't."

"Oh." Silence hovered for a while. "So Indians used

to live in these cabins? I read somewhere that before whites pushed them off their land, they used to burn little clearings like this to grow berries and tempt moose, and then hunt them. They were so good at burning small clearings without the fire getting out of control, they trained lots of white settlers in forest-fire fighting. I did a paper on that in school when I lived in Chilliwack."

"Mmm. And where did they all go?" Jake asked.

"Smallpox got lots of them."

Jake rose to peer into the rusty stove. Nothing there. He stuffed a waterproof pack in front of the broken window.

"They used to smoke fish for the canneries, or guide white hunters. The women made moccasins and gloves."

"Some still make a living trapping, I think," Jake offered. "I dunno. We'll ask Nancy to stop at the Prince George museum on the way back. Anyway, I suppose the grandkids or great-grandkids of who-ever lived here are still around. This is reserve land, you know. I guess in the States you would call it a reservation."

Peter nodded. "Either way, it means we're trespass-ing."

"Heck yes, but does this place look like it's been lived in for a while? Anyhow, I didn't see any five-star hotels on the way here, did you? If anyone comes round, we'll tell 'em what we've been through."

"Jake?"

"Yes, Peter."

"Someone *has* been here recently. I'm sure I saw a new oar leaning against our cabin."

Jake fell silent for a moment, then switched on his flashlight and moved toward the door. It was pitch-black outside now, but his light cut through the wet forest. He walked slowly around the cabin, to the drip-dripping of rain and croaking of frogs. His feet squelched small pine cones underfoot as he rounded one corner of the cabin and padded toward the next. He nearly bumped into the heavy wooden oar propped against a mossy wall. As he directed his light on the oar's shiny veneer, his pulse quickened. A Sam's Adventure Tours oar! An oar from the raft Ron had gone over the falls in. An oar belonging to the damaged raft they'd secured just the day before. He lowered the light to a plastic pail beneath it and crouched to examine two of the fattest pink salmon he'd ever seen. They smelled very fresh and clearly would not have been left alone long by forest animals.

Jake's shrunken stomach went to battle with his conscience. If a fisherman was camping in the abandoned village, he'd be back soon, and wouldn't be pleased to meet white trespassers, especially if they'd stolen his catch. On the other hand, Jake and Peter weren't about to head back out into the rain, especially given Peter's shoulder. They'd paddled fifty-five miles of super-intense stuff in two days with very little to eat. And wasn't the whole idea of hurrying down the canyon to find help?

Jake clicked off his flashlight, stuffed it into his wetsuit, and plunged his hands into the bucket. He was hungry enough to eat them right there, raw, but he would try and cook them over a fire in the rusted stove. As his hands closed around the slippery, smelly fish, footsteps sounded behind him and a flashlight beam landed on his hands. The light moved accusingly up and down his body until it spotlighted his face.

"What d'ya think you're doing?" growled a boy's voice.

16   Moses

"*M*oses?" Jake ventured.

"Yes, it's me, but what are *you* doing here? I thought you were on that fancy raft trip," came the gruff reply.

"Come inside and we'll explain everything." Jake, face a little flushed, let go of the fish. Moses tossed three more into the pail and followed Jake through the doorway, where the three boys spilled their respective stories. As it turned out, the driver Nancy had hired to shuttle the company bus to The Forks was Moses' uncle. He and Moses' father had decided to drop the bus five days early to backpack from The Forks to a favorite fishing spot in the canyon. They'd invited Moses along, parked the bus two mornings ago, and hiked to the abandoned village, where they'd camped for two nights. Then Moses, who wasn't big on long hikes, had asked permission to stay at the camp three more nights before walking back to the bus and catching a ride home with the rafters. Moses' father and uncle had agreed and hiked on upstream, intending to camp and fish for several days before cutting east and meeting Moses back home.

"But I thought there weren't any trails into the canyon," Jake said.

"None that most people know of," said Moses with a glint in his eyes.

"And where did you find the oar?"

"Just below Blender, of course. It's miles north before the canyon walls let you get close to the river again. That's a well-traveled oar if it came off the raft way back at the falls."

"Yes," said Jake, hanging his head. Going over the details of Ron's death again had made his eyes sting with the effort to hold back tears. Moses, though he hadn't known Ron, allowed for a few moments of silence.

"How'd you fare from that swim at team trials, anyway?" Peter asked. "Nasty hole you tangled with. Are you okay?"

"It was no big deal, just a cool new scar. Now, who wants grilled salmon for supper?"

"Me!" the walls echoed. A short while later, the three lit into a fantastic dinner, Jake and Moses smiling at Peter's attempts to eat one-armed. As the last of the food disappeared, Peter lay back and sighed. "Now all we need is a television and a bucket of ice cream."

Moses grabbed his tattered backpack and dug

through its contents. Out flew woolen socks, thermals, an impressive pocketknife, fishing lures, fishing line, and a chocolate bar. Peter and Jake licked their lips at the sight of this last item. Moses, digging deeper for more chocolate bars, looked startled as his hands closed around something else. Slowly, he pulled out a cellphone and stared at it. The other boys' mouths dropped open in disbelief.

"I forgot my dad left his phone with me. I guess you could use this, eh?" There was dead silence for a moment. Then Jake grabbed the phone and moved outside to dial emergency services.

Peter sat with Moses in awkward silence. He'd always felt uncomfortable around this sullen boy who rarely spoke when they were training together in Chilliwack. And yet here they had just shared an amazing meal and talked like old friends. But with Jake out of the room, Peter found he could only stare at Moses' expressionless face, trying to think of something to say. When the words did come blurting out, he regretted them instantly. "A cellphone. You Indians have come a long way from berry harvesting and moose hunting."

Moses, his mask-like face unbroken, surveyed Peter head to toe with dark-brown, intelligent eyes.

"And you've come a long way from covered wagons," he returned, the hint of a smile on his curled lip.

Peter's eyebrows shot up. He felt his cheeks redden. Finally, he relaxed and began to chuckle. The chuckle turned into a laugh as Moses joined in and the two dove for the chocolate bar.

"Shhh," Jake admonished from outside the door.

Jake was explaining the location of the stranded rafting party and Angus's condition to a medic who would be lifted in by helicopter. Next Peter heard him talking to his mother, and then Sam. To Peter's surprise, Jake handed the phone to Moses near the end of that conversation. Moses made some complicated arrangements with Sam, then phoned someone in his village. As it turned out, the Band Council ran a small commercial river-rafting operation that Sam was hiring to run down the Cattibone to retrieve the three rafts and any gear too heavy for the helicopters to bring out.

"We'll pay you back for all these calls," Peter offered as Moses put away his phone.

Moses laughed. "Don't worry. Your troubles are turning out to be big business for the Band."

"How's that?"

"Well, Sam's insurance will pay our rafting outfit to retrieve the rafts, and the provincial rescue services will pay the Band's helicopter company to fetch Angus and the passengers. And to think my father, who runs the helicopter service, is off fishing during all this!"

"Speaking of excitement," said Peter, "does anyone mind if we close down this party and get some shut-eye? This day has been way too long for me." The others agreed, unrolled their sleeping bags — Moses fetching his from his tent nearby — and crawled into the bunks. With the phone calls made and evacuation arranged, Peter knew he'd sleep soundly that night.

The next morning, after a delicious breakfast of oatmeal and berries courtesy of Moses' supplies, the boys tackled the question of how to get to The Forks. Peter knew his shoulder wasn't healed enough to let him paddle but he still made a half-hearted offer to kayak for the remaining twenty miles, which Nancy had said were Class 1 $^1/_2$. His shoulder was throbbing like a wound but part of him didn't want to break up the team he and Jake had become. That would have left Moses to make his way back on the trail. He'd arrive a few hours behind them even if he jogged.

"I'm no jogger," Moses admitted. "I suppose that's why I've never made the Canadian team. And since there's no real hurry now that we've done the phone calls, and Peter obviously isn't up to paddling, why don't I walk out with Peter? That way he won't get lost and I have some company. And it gives me lots of time to educate him. He needs some educating. Jake can paddle alone, using a rescue rope to tug the second kayak behind him like a caboose."

"That sounds like a strange form of resistance training," Jake complained. "Are you sure the rapids are mild from here to The Forks?"

"I've done them a million times. They're like stroking through syrup after the canyon. Mostly flat and boring, though the current moves along. You'll be safe on your own, but it'll take you till suppertime with your load. You'll beat Peter and me, but not by much. You'll have just enough time to take a nap before we show up. I'll chuck a few lightweight things into the extra kayak so I can carry that heavy oar of yours. You can't handle the weight of that even if we figured out a way to lash it on."

"Or we could leave the oar and extra kayak for the Band rafts to pick up," Peter suggested.

"I wouldn't risk it," said Moses. "This site sees visitors now and then, and they're not all honest. An oar and kayak are worth a bit."

"Anyway," said Peter, "Jake needs the extra weight for his kayak race training. Thanks to my shoulder, I've been demoted from his rival at the World Championships to his private coach." It was only just starting to sink in that he would be missing his own Nationals, but Peter decided that, for once, he was going to be a good sport.

"No way are you coaching me, you bossy motor-mouth," Jake shot back with a smile. Peter smiled too, knowing that Jake understood his keen disappointment, and that their pretend exchange of insults was really a sign of their renewed respect for one another.

"Oh yeah?" he responded. "Well, Moses and I are going to make you do thirty push-ups right here and now if you don't get moving! Race you to The Forks!"

"Neither The Forks nor the Nationals seem important anymore," Jake admitted. "I feel like I've just won the World Championships."

As Moses had promised, the riffles between Blender and The Forks were trivial, arduous, and bone-achingly long. Jake's thumb blisters had long since popped and his paddle was rubbing the red and raw remains of his hands. His back and shoulder muscles screamed from their two days' punishment, and Jake cursed the pull of the second kayak. At least he had a fat lunch to feast on midday, thanks to Moses, though no amount of food seemed to fill him since he'd entered the canyon.

Never had Jake seen such a welcome sight as the bridge over the river at The Forks. "Been nice to know ya," he shouted at the Cattibone, as he shouldered one boat up the bank to the bus and returned for the other.

The sweltering afternoon offered two choices. One was to sit in a bus whose stale air felt suffocating and whose worn vinyl seats burned his bottom. The other was to sit under the bridge with his feet thrust into the cold river, reading a dog-eared paperback novel Kate had left sitting in the bus. So he lost himself in that, dozing off now and then, until the afternoon heat let up and he heard the bus's horn honking. He scrambled up the bank to see Peter sitting in the driver's seat, and Moses strapping the oar onto the roof racks.

"How's the shoulder?" Jake asked.

"If it absolutely has to go for a walk, it prefers flat ground and well-groomed trails, neither of which Moses found much of," Peter complained. "But it's way better than last night, and probably in a heckuva lot better shape than if I'd tried to paddle twenty miles. Your sling made it tolerable, anyway."

"So that means I can pull a few three-sixties in this vehicle on the way home?" Moses joked.

"Can you drive?" Jake asked, hopefully.

"Can I drive? Of course I can drive! I've driven snowmobiles, dirt bikes, jet skis, power boats, tractors, helicopters — as a co-pilot with my dad — and race cars."

"Where have you driven race cars?" asked Peter, dumbfounded.

"On video games with simulated controls. I reckon it's the same thing. We'll soon find out, anyways. Keys, please."

17   The Reunion

Moses had managed to keep the bus on the wide, empty road for one hundred miles when they came across a party of hitchhikers at dusk.

"Stop for them," Jake ordered Moses. "That's Jim and his gang."

And so it was. The tired, filthy hikers climbed aboard, pleased to see Jake and Peter alive and well, and the two groups pooled their stories. Once Kate had dropped them off on the far shore above the waterfall, Jim and his buddies had pointed their compasses due east and endured uninspiring conditions for three days: blankets of mosquitoes, close encounters with snakes, and impassable cliffs requiring lengthy detours into swampy terrain. They had even surprised a moose, who'd forced them to scramble up trees and stay there for much of an afternoon. A wide stream had also slowed them. They'd ended up lashing together fallen trees to form a makeshift raft, but

Derek had fallen in halfway across nonetheless.

"Let's just say it was an adventure for a noble cause," said Jim. "Your Band really should cut a trail across the Reserve into the canyon, Moses, at least for emergencies."

"There's a thought," Moses replied, winking at his companions. Despite the fun he'd clearly had weaving back and forth across the road, Moses handed the driving over to Jim with a cheerful, "Canadians drive on the right side of the road. Let me know if you need any instruction."

Half an hour later, the bus pulled up outside the Reserve's community center, and seven adventurers filed off it in the dark. Moses' rotund mother, Doreen Wilson, met them at the community center door with open arms and a glowing smile. She ushered them to a long table laden with fresh-baked bannock and homemade blueberry jam.

"Help yourselves while I cook you up some real supper," she said. "And set an extra place, Moses. We've got company."

The boys paid no attention to her last comment until a tall, muscular figure stepped into the doorway and looked them over with a wry smile. Jake's knife clattered to his plate. Peter's face went as pasty as bread dough.

"Hey kid," a voice said softly as the man sauntered over. "The only thing I have to say is, don't drink and drive. Especially when there are logs on the road."

Jake couldn't bring himself to move. Not after last seeing Ron cloaked in white and rising from a whirlpool. Not after watching him crash over the lip of a waterfall he could not possibly have survived. Not after all the tears he'd spent, and all the blame he'd piled on Peter for the tragedy.

"R-r-ron . . . ?" he stammered "But how . . . ?"

Ron moved to the table and gripped Jake's shoulders fondly before he sat down. "When I went off the falls, I hit the water like a knife diving through lemon meringue pie." He grinned and paused for effect, then pulled a tin of tobacco out of his borrowed shirt pocket and inserted a pinch in his mouth.

"The force took me down several leagues, or so it seemed. I s'pose I'm damned lucky the water beneath the falls is so deep — and clear where I torpedoed in. Anyhow, soon as I stopped plunging, I turned myself round in a panic and started flappin' arms and legs to head up. Like Superman flying for the top of a skyscraper," he embellished, pulling on his chin hairs and flashing his blue eyes around the table to ensure everyone was listening.

"It's the only time in my life I've prayed," he reflected. "I never saw no light, like you do when you're caught in a hole and swimming for the little yellow bubbles on the surface. I figured I was done for when I felt my lungs about to pop and I still couldn't see light. 'Course, I came up under the flipped raft, and my life jacket kept my head above water, but I was so whacked out, so sure I wasn't gonna make it, it took me a while to figure out I was alive 'n' breathin' and under the stupid boat. I thought I heard some voices, but for all I knew, they were angels' voices come to fetch me to heaven.

"Well, okay," he corrected himself. "Devils' voices come to take me the other way. Whatever . . ." He took a long chew on his tobacco and spit into a nearby plate. He scratched his oily hair and tugged on his ponytail while his rapt audience waited.

"Finally, I got it together to get mad at the rubber tube that kept knockin' into my head, draggin' me along. I pushed on the roof, but it wouldn't flop over. So I took a breath and dived under and grabbed onto the outer tube. By then I was in that freaky narrows, with waves leaping off the walls and pulling the raft every which way. So I kicked and lifted myself up onto the raft bottom, and floated outta that mess on the upside-down raft. That put me right into the canyon, which was really kickin', and it was gettin' too dark to see where we were headed. So I did what every good raft guide is taught in guide school: I grabbed the side ropes and flopped the raft back upright. Just like a wind surfer. That made me fall back into the river, 'course, but I got myself pulled back aboard just as the raft hit hard on a rock and punctured its front right chamber. I jumped to the high side and made that thing back off the rock, though I couldn't see where we were goin' next. Then I notice a rescue rope trailin' off the back, draggin' along a small tree trunk, of all the stupid things. Someone will have to explain that to me some day.

"I took hold of the rope and hauled in the log, and used it like a spear to stop us crashin' into more boulders. I saved that raft's skin a good dozen times; we fought the canyon pretty near half the night. When the moon came up, things got better. I could see pretty good. But the river got us eventually. Somewhere — who knows where — the raft flipped again, and I got tossed into the drink beyond reach. I got knocked 'round good between there and whatever eddy saved my pretty little arse. Then I crawled outta the water — I was two degrees above froze — and went to sleep, wetsuit and all on the beach. I slept and hung out all the next day, expectin' someone to come by and rescue me. I was up in the woods feeding my face with berries when I see Jake and Peter goin' by, hell-bent on winnin' the Olympics or something. I shouted, but you guys didn't see or hear me." He reached out a big hand to mock-cuff Jake and Peter.

"That's when I knew something was up, that the rafts might not be coming and the kayaks had been sent for help. Including *my* kayak," he said, clearing his throat as Peter produced a thin smile and turned to study a smudge on the windowpane.

"But I waited the rest of the afternoon just in case the rafts were right behind and slept the night under a ledge in the rain. Next morning, I'm decidin' I gotta hike out, when imagine my surprise. Two fishermen walk up, just like that. Moses' dad and uncle, turns out. They perk me up with the best damn coffee I've had and fry me up some fish. Then they walk me all the way back here on a wild trail I'd never've known was a trail if they hadn't been leadin'. It took the rest of that day plus most of today; we camped along the trail last night and got here two hours ago. Doreen here's become my best friend since, eh dear? Nonstop bannock and jam. What I really wanna know, though, is how is Angus?"

"He's going to be fine," said Nancy, who'd just appeared in the doorway, trailed by Kate, Vinay, the Joshis, and Montpetits. Nancy walked over to Ron and despite his embarrassed protests, gave him a long, firm hug. Doreen Wilson hustled in with a plateful of fried chicken, popped her hand over her mouth and said, "Oh dear. Back to the kitchen. What is this, a convention or something?"

Nancy rested her arm on Jake's shoulder. "After Moses' dad got home here and phoned into his chopper office, his partner — the pilot who rescued us — was thoughtful enough to page us at the hospital to let us know about Ron. He even gave us a ride here, as you can see. So Angus is in good hands and the gang's all here safe and happy, thanks to Jake and Peter. Of course, all passengers will receive a full refund."

"We don't want a refund," Jim piped up. "We've had the adventure of our lives, the best combination rafting/hiking trip Canada can offer. Right boys?"

"Righto!" Patrick agreed. "Sign us up for the next one!"

"And we wouldn't dream of taking any money back," said Richard Montpetit, locking his arms around Peter, "especially after the helicopter pilot showed me around his machine; he even let me fly for a few minutes. This has been a *great* rafting/helicopter adventure. As for Peter, it goes without saying that kayaking the Cattibone was his dream, even if it was never in the plan."

"And you've got to admit, it has been the most memorable anniversary we'll ever have," Laura Montpetit chipped in, planting a kiss on her son's head that turned his face crimson.

"We agree," Sunil Joshi insisted, his arms around Anita and Neeta. "Neeta has already asked us to book another adventure trip with Vin … I mean, with Sam's Adventure Tours. In fact, I'm in awe of how everyone pitched in to turn things around. I only wish I'd been able to do more for Angus."

As Peter managed to pry himself loose from his parents' arms, he turned to Nancy.

"Nancy, when my shoulder is better, is there any chance you need another slave for this adventure company of yours? I realize I don't seem the best candidate, given the trouble I've caused, but I've turned over a new leaf. Anyway, I'm strong and have tons of energy, and I need a job." He drew himself up tall, and directed a gaze at his startled parents. "I want to start paying for my own stuff."

Nancy looked from Peter to his parents, and from Peter to Jake and back again.

"Well," she said. "Sam has been talking about adding some backcountry heli-ski and snowboard tours into our lineup, and your parents tell me you're an ace snowboarder. So there's spring break to consider. But I don't suppose you'd want to do a winter adventure?"

Shortly after Jake returned to Chilliwack, he traveled to Ontario for the Canadian National Championships with a carload of Canadian team members. At first, he was quiet around them, nervous the way he'd always been when thrown together with these cocky, talented paddlers, but then he reminded himself he was one of them — he'd made the team.

His shyness began melting away when they peppered him with questions about the Cattibone, and let him know they were very jealous of his adventures there. To his surprise, he soon found himself jabbering freely, even initiating arm wresting contests at lunch stops. He quickly decided they were all okay, not the least bit stuck up like he'd always thought. It gradually dawned on him that they had never been snobbish; he was the one who had shied away from them for fear they thought he wasn't good enough for them. Now that he was making more effort to banish the grumpiness that he had been wearing like a smelly T-shirt for too long — okay, so Peter was right about that — he could see that they were great guys, fun to be around. Guys with their own insecure moments, guys who needed encouragement now and again as much as he did.

Even before they reached Ontario and began training together, he could feel his fellow team members drawing him out. He could feel a new "Jake" sprouting from the Jake that had existed before the Cattibone trip. A Jake who joked and laughed and took full part in the discussions of race strategy. He couldn't remember a time he'd felt so light and free. Well, he could, and it had to do with when his dad had still been around, and Peter had been his best buddy. For the first time in years, he was willing to let the old Jake come out and play.

When they arrived at the pre-Nationals training sessions, he was excited to see Peter, who'd flown out with his dad. Peter burst onto the scene with his usual enthusiasm, wearing a bright red sling that he got all the paddlers — especially the girls — to sign. And yet, throughout the grueling workouts, Jake found that Peter hardly left his side. Though at first Jake had to force himself to be gracious about it, deep down, he really appreciated Peter's bang-on advice about how to tackle certain gates, and his newfound loyalty, borne of a new bond between them. He also couldn't help noticing a new Peter: a Peter who coached him out of earshot of the other team members and refused to take any credit when Jake did thank him in front of the other guys. And when the guys asked Peter about the Cattibone, he always drew Jake into telling most of the tales, as if he himself had barely been along for the ride.

Thanks to Peter's coaching and their time on the Cattibone, Jake felt stronger and surer of himself with each training session. When the big morning arrived, the day his division raced, he felt as ready as he'd ever been, capable of tearing up the course.

And tear it up he did: fast and clean on both runs, juice pumping from his arms like he'd invented the sport. When his name was called to stand on the highest platform of the awards podium, he looked down at a sea of faces that seemed genuinely happy for him. He also sensed that only one face looked completely unsurprised: Peter's.

Happy as he was to touch the medal hanging around his chest, however, Jake had to admit that the most thrilling moment was when a sponsor approached him to offer him a hot new kayak for free. For free. Something he hadn't imagined in his wildest dreams.

When he phoned home to tell his mother and Alyson, he learned that Neeta had won an award for her magazine photo of the waterfall jump but, at Peter's request, had refused to identify the paddler in it. He also learned that Sam's Adventure Tours was holding a party the next day to celebrate Angus's release from hospital.

Jake had to smile at the Canadian team's astonishment when he and Peter turned down the after-Nationals partying to catch a flight with Peter's dad so they could return to Chilliwack. How could they be expected to understand? How could anyone who had not been down the Cattibone grasp what was really worth celebrating?

As he and Peter climbed into Richard Montpetit's airport rental van, they waved until they thought their wrists would fall off. They were happy waves. Waves they could repeat anytime they liked, race after race. Waves were good, especially when they were white-water river waves. Waves of danger and challenge that had turned into waves of friendship — and trust.

Acknowledgements

I'm particularly indebted to Dr. Martin Blackwell, MD, for helping me craft medical crises; Bob Rutherford of Prince George, B.C., for his caving expertise; and Russ Brown of Chilliwack River Rafting in B.C. for updating me on river raft guiding. Thanks also to Ted and Nancy Hill, my "ornithologists on call," as well as Dr. Manish D. Joshi, Venkat Ramen, Dr. Bruce Miller of the University of British Columbia's anthropology department, and the Fraser–Fort George Regional Museum.

I'd like to acknowledge three youths who read early drafts — Andrew Macfarlane, Rose McPhilemy, and David Rawcliffe — and two "grown-up" friends who did the same: Scott Shipley and Ann-Marie Metten.

I'd like to acknowledge Leona Trainer, the hardest working and most cheerful of all literary agents. And, of course, Robert McCullough, Leanne McDonald, Robin Rivers, Carolyn Bateman, Sophie Hunter, Claire Wilson, and the rest of the talented staff at Whitecap Books, who made it all happen from there.

Past and present members of my kids' whitewater kayaking club, Paddling Punks, please note that any resemblance you bear to Raging River characters is purely coincidental.

Last, but not least, a hug to my husband, Steve, fellow whitewater aficionado.

PHOTO BY PETER LAU

About the Author

Pam Withers has worked as a whitewater raft guide, kayak instructor, journalist, editor, and associate publisher. She has kayaked the Colorado River through the Grand Canyon. A former associate editor of *Adventure Travel* magazine in New York City, Pam was born in Wisconsin. She has since lived in the Dakotas, California, and Washington state, as well as in England and Ireland. She currently makes her home in Vancouver, British Columbia, with her husband and son, where she enjoys cross-country skiing and kayaking when she's not writing and editing business books or working on her young adult novels.

Look for the next book in the *Take It to the Extreme* series, when Jake, Peter and Moses tackle a backcountry heli-skiing and snowboarding adventure in *Peak Survival*. For more information on the series, check out <u>www.takeittotheextreme.com</u>